"I think I need to explain something here,"

he said. "I'm just not ready for any kind of commitment."

Amanda pondered that a moment. The telephone line fairly hummed with Cole's breathing. "So? I don't remember either of us saying anything about ropes, strings or marriage. Engagement, even."

"You don't have to say it. Permanence, home and slippers sticks out all over you like a neon sign."

"If you'd take a good look at that neon sign, you'd notice it was off. Besides, I think it wise to get to know someone before contemplating marriage."

"Good," Cole said with confidence. "Considering our reactions to each other in the past, I think the wise, adult thing to do is stay out of each other's way."

Amanda gritted her teeth. "I couldn't agree more."

Dear Reader,

Although our culture is always changing, the desire to love and be loved is a constant in every woman's heart. Silhouette Romances reflect that desire, sweeping you away with books that will make you laugh and cry, poignant stories that will move you time and time again.

This year we're featuring Romances with a playful twist. Remember those fun-loving heroines who always manage to get themselves into tricky predicaments? You'll enjoy reading about their escapades in Silhouette Romances by Brittany Young, Debbie Macomber, Annette Broadrick and Rita Rainville.

We're also publishing Romances by many of your all-time favorites such as Ginna Gray, Dixie Browning, Laurie Paige and Joan Hohl. Your overwhelming reaction to these authors has served as a touchstone for us, and we're pleased to bring you more books with Silhouette's distinctive medley of charm, wit and—above all—*romance*. I hope you enjoy this book, and the many stories to come.

Sincerely,

Rosalind Noonan
Senior Editor
SILHOUETTE BOOKS

CURTISS ANN MATLOCK
Crosswinds

Silhouette *Romance*

Published by Silhouette Books New York

America's Publisher of Contemporary Romance

With thanks to The Person in charge,
and Robin Kaigh

SILHOUETTE BOOKS
300 E. 42nd St., New York, N.Y. 10017

ISBN: 0-373-08422-6

First Silhouette Books printing March 1986

Books by Curtiss Ann Matlock

Silhouette Special Edition
A Time and a Season #275

Silhouette Romance
Crosswinds #422

CURTISS ANN MATLOCK

loves to travel and has lived in eight different states, from Alaska to Florida. Sixteen years ago she married her high school sweetheart and inspiration, James. The Matlocks are now settled in Oklahoma, where Curtiss is concentrating on being a homemaker and writer. Other time is taken up with gardening, canning, crocheting and, of course, reading. "I was probably born with a book in hand."

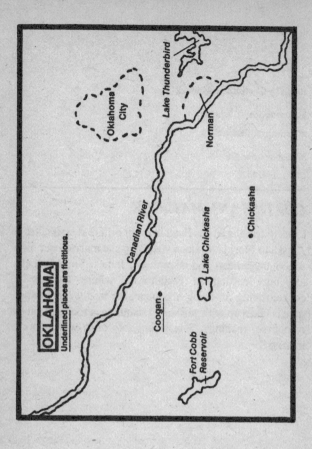

OKLAHOMA

Underlined places are fictitious.

Canadian River

Oklahoma City

Lake Thunderbird

Norman

Coogan

Lake Chickasha

Chickasha

Fort Cobb Reservoir

Chapter One

Amanda Jameson was in her office at the church when she first caught the scent. She was tilted back in the old oak chair she'd padded with a pillow, her feet propped inelegantly upon the desk. A blank sheet of paper glaring in the light from the desk lamp mocked her. She'd been trying to think, to write, but not one single thought would form. Tossing her pencil to the desk top in disgust, Amanda stuck out her tongue at the offending paper.

Her gaze traveled to a lone yellow rose sticking from a bud vase at the edge of her desk. A gift from a young bride that morning. Remembering the woman's radiant face, Amanda smiled, then something within her heart squeezed and an intense longing she couldn't understand or even name swept over her.

Paul. Memories of him flooded back. They had been exceedingly frequent since she'd received that letter from Mira Shaw. Mira had run into Paul at the Paris airport in the spring. There'd not been time for a real conversation, Mira had written, just hello and you look good. Mira wondered had Amanda been in touch with Paul.

No, Amanda thought ruefully, that was over years ago. Amanda gave a half chuckle. Over? How could something be over when it had never begun?

For a brief moment the image of a dark-haired man she'd seen at Tate's Garage that afternoon appeared in her thoughts. She'd seen only his back as he slipped into a sleek black pickup. The set of his shoulders had caught her attention, their movement suggesting strength tempered with ease and harmony.

Harmony. How odd a word to use, she thought, musing over the term in connection with a man's physique. But that was what had come to mind when she'd seen the fluid way he moved as he slipped into the seat of his truck.

"Oh, for heaven's sake!" she whispered. Why was she thinking about men so much lately? Be honest, she teased herself, and the old wooden chair creaked as she impatiently rearranged her small feet on the desk. It was his truck that caught your eye, Manda Jameson. You do have an eye for sporty rugged vehicles.

The truck was indeed eye-catching, with its polished mirror finish and gleaming chrome. She'd noticed it several times in the past month or so. It wasn't as easy to admit she was curious about the driver as well, had tried, but never succeeded, in getting a good look at him.

The image of the man's strong shoulders again floated across her mind. With an impatient gesture, Amanda brushed wisps of hair from her forehead as if to brush away confusing thoughts at the same time.

A light cooling breeze stirred through the open window, bringing a hint of humidity. But only a hint. There was something there—something. Amanda stilled, her senses tuned, then relaxed. It must have been imagination.

It was dusk, the end of a blistering hot late-August day in rural Oklahoma. Coral rays of the setting sun lit the sky, and trees stood out like black silhouettes on orange silk. Cicadas and crickets had begun their full-fledged orchestration. Martins darted about, feeding on mosquitoes. From the distance came the faint sound of a train whistle.

Gazing west, Amanda prayed the purple band stretched above the horizon to the northwest that she hoped would prove to be rain clouds—clouds which came and hovered over the land and dumped barrels—lakes even—of water.

There had been no measurable rain for three months, a not too uncommon happening in central Oklahoma, but it was wearing on the farming community of Coogan. People seemed to watch the skies with ever-increasing expectancy. How long could it remain dry? Amanda was beginning to believe forever.

Faintly the breeze again stirred the blinds. It struck her then. A familiar scent wafted past, was gone, then came again. Icy fingers of dread clutched at her spine while her mind urged caution. Half-cocking her head, Amanda stilled and waited, her sense of smell testing the breeze.

And faintly it came once more. The acrid odor of smoke, the smell of fire.

Immediately, in one fluid movement, Amanda was on her feet and out the office door. She ran through the tall-ceilinged sanctuary and into the entrance hall, scrambling up the ladder that led to the old-fashioned steeple above. From there she knew she could see for miles.

She worked to slide the heavy trapdoor aside, then pulled herself up to peer over the sidewall of the small steeple. There wasn't much room—just enough for Amanda to squeeze her slight frame past the bell and hold herself up by the rim of the sidewall.

Instinctively she looked south, her eyes searching the darkly shadowed woods and meadows of the rolling hills. Seeing nothing, she again carefully combed her gaze across the land.

A bright flicker caught her eye. It licked at the sky and then, almost like a streak of orange lightning, zipped wide, forming a line.

Grass fire.

Amanda had seen them before. With the light breeze, it might just be a nuisance; if the wind rose, it would be an extremely dangerous threat. It was perhaps a mile, maybe two, to the south. How far it had already burned, Amanda couldn't tell, but even as she watched, the orange splotch on the darkened land widened. It was coming north, pushed ahead by a southerly breeze.

The grass was dry—so very dry—and tall. Roy Hammond had not grazed cattle there this year. In fact, Amanda guessed, he had probably been planning to cut and bale the large section in the coming weeks.

Her pulse beat loud in her ears as her eyes skimmed west, assessing the danger. There were several small wooded areas and trees along fence rows, then Hammond's hay barn, half full. Farther up, though Amanda couldn't see it for a rise in the land, was the Hammonds' house, and nearby were the Carters' and Seifs'.

Her eyes skimmed east. There was Coogan Road, a wide country road of clay dirt scraped into the earth—the same road that ran in front of the church. Brush and trees grew thick on either side, fuel for the fire to feed on.

And there was nothing between the fire and the church but acres and acres of dry pasture edged with assorted brush, scrub oak and sumac.

Amanda lowered herself, struggled hastily with the heavy door, then felt her way as quickly as possible down the ladder in the darkness. Pushing away the alarming thoughts which threatened to take over, she forced her mind to think of what to do first, then second. She couldn't get to third.

The community of Coogan, just down the hill from the church, was simply a wide spot at the intersection of two state highways. It boasted a combination gas station, garage and café known simply as Tate's, a small grocery store, and an old one-room schoolhouse, now used for a community center. The nearest official fire department was fifteen miles away.

Reaching the telephone, Amanda pressed her hand to her head and sought the Hammonds' number from memory. She dialed with fingers grown clumsy with apprehension.

"Mary," she said when the familiar voice answered, "there's a grass fire to the south in your pasture—near the railroad tracks."

Mary Hammond gave a sharp intake of breath, and Amanda listened as she relayed the information to Roy who was obviously nearby. There came the muffle of excited voices and the scrape of chairs in the background.

"Amanda—" it was Roy Hammond now, his voice clipped and sure "—where and how big?"

"About straight south from your house, this side of the tracks. Can't see how far west. Looks small, just started, Roy, but you know..." Amanda's voice trailed off. She certainly didn't need to be telling Roy Hammond about grass fires.

"Okay. I'll call down to Tate's and round up some help. You call over to the Binger fire station." Roy barked out the instructions, then was gone, leaving the dial tone buzzing in Amanda's ear.

Fire station, fire station. The words whirled in Amanda's head as she scanned the telephone book for the number, dialed and gave the needed information.

As she replaced the receiver, she paused and glanced around the room, thinking what one thing she would save—if it came to that.

No, she thought. It won't come to that. The church was old, so old it had a life, a breath of its own. It reflected the strengths and weaknesses of the people who had built it and attended it—three full generations. Mae Loggin had come here as a girl, and she was seventy now.

No, she repeated to herself as she strode from the building. It won't come to that.

In the light provided by a floodlamp at the corner of the white clapboard building, Amanda unwound the garden hose and stretched it the length of the churchyard to the barbed-wire fence of the pasture, to be ready if needed. The dry tall grass and black-eyed Susans of the fence row, usually so lovely to look at, now appeared monstrously threatening. An ancient elm stood at the corner. Its wide canopy of branches hung low, its leaves silver in the lamplight—a perfect invitation to the flames should they reach this far.

Pausing, Amanda stared west, allowing her arms to drop to her sides. The breeze from the south seemed to be on the rise, the smell of smoke stronger. The sky was a pale creamy color toward the horizon, night-blue above. The band of purple to the northwest had expanded and was approaching.

"Please. Oh, please let those be rain clouds," Amanda whispered as she headed for her Jeep.

Cole Mattox banged on the dash with one hand and continued to steer with the other. He was driving north along a soft sandy-clay road, a shortcut home from Chickasha, where he'd just had his pickup's air conditioner repaired. At least supposedly. Ten minutes out of town, the darn thing had made a horrendous rattling noise, spit out several slivers of ice and then quit blowing completely.

Cole was an even-tempered man, and it took a lot to get him mad; he'd about reached his limit. His was a brand-new, top-of-the-line pickup and the dealer had promised satisfaction. And it was as Cole toyed with various ideas of how to get this satisfaction that he noticed the red glow to the sky on his northwest.

Immediately Cole guessed what it was. Born and raised in this country, he'd seen grass fires before, too many to count. Fire could be a friend, as it burned off unwanted weeds and plowed-over stumps—or it could be a treacherous uncontrollable enemy, eating up the land.

The glow seemed frightfully close to his home—maybe it was his place. Adrenalin sent blood pounding in his ears as Cole pressed on the accelerator, taking the steering wheel in both hands as the truck skidded back and forth over the soft sand. Topping a hill, he stopped for a better look. It was in Hammond's pasture, moving north, northeast. He could pick out headlights heading across the pasture toward the flames and was relieved the alert had gone out.

The wind was rising. If the fire reached the pasture edge, even the wide expanse of clay-dirt road wouldn't keep it from jumping across to the tall weeds and trees of Cole's farm.

In a split second he pictured the exposed frame of his newly begun house and his completed woodworking shop, a shop he'd built with his own muscle and sweat.

Again Cole determinedly pressed the accelerator, heading for his father's house, which was nearest, and the help and equipment he'd need. He prayed those brothers of his had decided to do something original like stay home on a Friday night.

Mae Loggin's eyes were drawn to the glowing sky to the west. "It looks almost like a sunrise," she breathed, her gaze fastened on the bright orange light that lit the sky.

Lowry nodded. "You take care out there, old woman."

"Humph," Mae retorted. "After forty-three years of marriage, old man, you ought to know I will. I may be getting old, but that doesn't mean stupid."

Lowry careened down Coogan Road, the dust of others before them billowing in the headlights. Mae held to the door handle and water sloshed from the two washtubs in the back as Lowry turned the pickup and bounced over the cattle-guard entrance to the pasture. Weeds tore at the sides of the truck. The headlights played across John Tidwell's truck in front of them, then Mae recognized Amanda Jameson's bright red Jeep. She wasn't at all surprised. Amanda could usually be found in the midst of things.

The truck's headlights illuminated Amanda, one foot in the Jeep, waving frantically. Stray wisps of honey-brown hair, windblown and damp from perspiration, framed her face, while the rest was pulled into her usual French braid and gathered at the nape of her neck. Her face was sooty, but her eyes shone with intensity.

"We have to pull back," Amanda cried. "It's coming too fast! Pull back!"

Lowry shifted and turned the truck. Mae half expected John Tidwell to stop and argue; he always did, but for once in the man's life, he didn't waste precious time.

They were a good crew. Mae recognized the Mattox brothers, a Hammond Ranch truck, Boyer's Jeep, the Thomases', and more trucks and people arriving every minute. All of them knew what it meant to battle a grass fire. With organized fire departments miles away from outlying communities, neighbor helped neighbor. It might be Roy Hammond's land burning now, but the fire could take the whole of Coogan with it, as well as acres and acres of other people's ranches.

With a battery lamp set atop the cab of the pickup, Mae joined Lowry in the back wetting sacks and blankets. Of course, she couldn't move as fast as she once had, but she and Lowry made a good team, she thought proudly as she handed out the wet sacks as fast as she could soak them. Lowry's heavy breathing worried her, but then he, like her, would rather end his time on his feet than in bed.

Moments later, the Thomases' truck pulled alongside, and Sheryl Thomas and her daughter began wetting sacks as well. There was a steady stream of workers—men, women and children—running from the trucks to the flames, beating them with the wet material or shoveling dirt.

Mae paused to scan the flames. In minutes the area they covered had widened. Not too big yet, though. Hopefully all the fire would take would be a few acres of grass. That they could spare. But lives were too precious.

Mae was a tiny woman, not over five feet, and lean, and as always, Amanda was struck by her vitality. Mae was scolding Amanda, as usual. Mae scolded everyone all the time, fire or no.

"You ought to know better," Mae hollered down as she took Amanda's half-dried and scorched blanket and pushed it into the washtub of water. "Get a pair of gloves from the seat. Go on now."

Amanda did as she was told. She was glad for the gloves, though they scratched going on over her heat-chapped hands. Wearing the same tailored slacks and short-sleeved blouse she'd had on that afternoon, she wasn't exactly dressed for fire fighting—but then, fires didn't wait for you to change.

For a moment, Amanda paused and looked over her shoulder toward the church. Sitting back from the road a good two hundred yards, its floodlight a beacon shining from the clapboard corner, it was smack in the fire's line. Bushes obscured the lower part of the church with its north and south wings. Bushes just right for burning and for sending sparks to the church's roof. The old buildings of Coogan flashed through her thoughts, and then her attention was drawn back to the immediate threat. Stepping to the back of Lowry's truck, she reached up to take a fresh wet sack from Mae.

Gene White stepped beside her. Sweating and breathing hard, he exchanged his sack for a wet one. His weathered face broke into a toothy grin. "Guess this makes you fully one of us, Amanda. Unless it changes your mind and you're going to hightail it out of here." He coughed into his hands, a raspy cough.

Amanda knew with Gene's age and health, he shouldn't be exposed to the smoke. But he wanted to do his part, needed to, just as all the others did.

"You can't get rid of me this easily, Gene," Amanda joked.

"Easily?" Gene's laugh was gravelly, and he shook his head as he headed back to the edge of the flames.

It looks rather like a sea of fire, Amanda thought. *No, a wide river.* The fiery strip was yards wide in some places and only several feet in others. Stretching from east to west, it left blackened ground behind as it burned.

Men, women and children fought the blaze. Amanda counted ten figures this side of the fire and knew more were gathered to the west. Some of the men used shovels, digging into the hard-packed ground and throwing the dirt to smother the blaze, trying also to make a trench as they went.

They didn't seek to put the fire out, so much as to contain it until it burned up its own fuel.

The one fire engine that had come—Old Red, Mae called it—sprayed water at the point of the fire jutting farthest north.

The wind, which seemed to be rising, pulled at Amanda's hair, bringing the crackling sound and acrid smell of the burning grass. Amanda was amazed at how quiet the fire was, though. It seemed to her something so turbulent as the flaming grass should make a lot of noise. It probably would if—when, Amanda decided, it reached the trees.

Contain it. That was the key. But everywhere it kept breaking through. As if alive it jumped, creating tiny little blazes of grass that burned together into larger sections in seconds. Amanda beat out one, and two more sprang up to the side of her—or behind her, causing her to have to step quickly around or even jump through to get out of the way. Smoke burned her lungs and scorched her eyes. Again and again she hit the flames with a vengeance, smacking at the little devils of fire that jumped farther and farther ahead with each small gust of wind. When her sack dried, she'd run back and wet it, again and again. She didn't know how long she'd been working, just that the flames still came.

Twice, they were forced to stop and move the vehicles from the reach of the flames. The second time, out onto the road.

Panting, her arms aching, Amanda stepped back to catch her breath. She brushed the perspiration from her forehead with the back of her hand and raised her eyes. She'd not realized the distance she'd traveled before the fire. It had now burned way over half the pasture, and she was very near the gate in the east fence.

The wind had remained low, and Amanda breathed a silent thanks. In the middle the fire was extinguished, but still

it burned on each end. Two more fire trucks had arrived,
trying to keep control of the west side of the fire, as it ate
into the brush and smaller trees of the wood and threatened
the Hammond hay barn.

Amanda heard a warning shout. A moment later the
brush to her left burst into flame. It was so very odd, much
like Moses's burning bush, Amanda thought idiotically as
she watched for a moment, wide-eyed, frozen in her surprise. Then she turned to retreat, but found the fire spread
to the taller scrub oaks behind her at the edge of the fence.
Suddenly it was all around her.

The flames crackled loudly, and clutching her now-dried
sack, she tried to shield her face from the intensifying heat
with her arm as she searched frantically for an escape route.
Fear welled in her throat, smoke choked her lungs, and her
vision blurred as tears stung her burning eyes.

There wasn't any time to think, only find the spot with the
shortest grass. Covering her face with both arms, she pre-
pared to jump through the wall of fire when she felt herself
lifted around the waist by strong arms. A wet gunnysack was
thrown over her head and she was carried rather like a fifty-
pound bag of dog food.

The next instant, Amanda found herself just the other
side of the pasture gate, sitting sideways upon a man's lap
as he lost his balance, and they both toppled to the ground.

She fumbled to free her head from the disgusting wet sack
and take a good clean breath. Coughing and sputtering, she
tried to open eyelids which felt dry as sandpaper.

"Well, I'll be damned…" the man said, his voice so deep
that it vibrated.

Amanda coughed and gave a half laugh. "Oh, I don't
think so," she managed before coughing again. She got her
eyes open then, and looked straight into the man's face. It
was extremely close to hers. The golden light of the fire

glinted off cheeks covered by a soft dark beard and mustache. His eyes were the color of chocolate, and they shimmered before Amanda as her vision blurred with tears.

For a split second, they stared at one another, dumbfounded: he, either because she was a woman or because she was a little slip of a person, which she knew she was; and she, because it had all happened so fast and because he was terribly handsome and she was sitting rather intimately on his lap.

"Are you all right?" he demanded gruffly, his rough hands holding her bare upper arms. "Not burned or anything?" He raked a hand over her hair and across her shoulder, as if searching for smoldering embers.

Amanda shook her head. "No...no. Scorched, maybe, but I'm okay."

"Amanda? Cole?" It was Mae's voice and Amanda struggled to see her through eyes which still teared. "You all right? Lord, what we all thought when we saw you two falling out of that fire."

Amanda felt arms helping her rise. She sat on the tailgate of Lowry's truck, and Mae pressed a cool wet towel to her face. "The fire..." Amanda pushed the cloth away.

"Looks like we've got it licked now," a familiar low voice rumbled. Again the cocoa eyes regarded her, seeming even darker in the low light supplied by Lowry's lamp.

Following his gaze, Amanda stared at the pasture. Is it over, she asked herself, hesitating, tense. The lone fire truck, Old Red, moved slowly toward them, men spraying the flames where only moments ago Amanda had been standing. Smoke twirled upward, illuminated by the fire truck's headlights. They couldn't see how it went now to the west, but a golden glow still tinged the sky—perhaps Hammond's hay barn.

"Your place is out of danger now, Cole," Lowry said.

"Uh-huh." Amanda felt the man's weight as he relaxed against the tailgate and took a drink from the cup Mae handed him. Other figures, silhouettes in the darkness, gathered around Lowry's truck. It was quiet, with only a few murmurs. A thread of tension ran deep and everyone watched, waiting to see if one lone spark still lived to start up again.

Slipping to the ground, Amanda stretched and turned her eyes up the hill toward the church. With the floodlight beacon, she could see the church's roof and the top of the tall windows. Then even as she watched, a flame burst along the fence row. A single spark—a loose piece of fiery grass or branch—had blown upward, and it was beginning again.

"Oh, my..." Amanda pointed, for the moment unable to say more.

She sprinted then for the Jeep, while all around her people leaped into action and engines started. The Jeep rocked as a tall figure vaulted into the seat beside her. His gaze raked her fleetingly, then he raised himself, held on to the windshield and began shouting orders for some to stay and others to follow. A truck sped up beside them. "Get over to Nate," the man beside Amanda called to the driver, "and see if he can get another fire truck over here."

Amanda shifted into gear and pressed the accelerator, speeding toward the church. Dust billowed around the Jeep, scratching at her eyes, but she ignored it. Not now, she thought, her being railing against the fire. Not when we'd almost won.

The fire crackled loudly as it shot down the fence row, amply fed by the tall dried weeds and scrub oak, the flames shooting into the black sky. The breeze picked up and swirled, sending the flames spreading once again into the dry grassy field. Amanda passed, giving it a wide berth, and drove into the churchyard.

Braking quickly, she jumped to the ground and headed for the tall handle of the pump. She sensed rather than saw the man racing behind her. He grabbed her arm and took the hose from her hand. "Get in the church and shut all the doors and windows—all of them!"

Without hesitation, Amanda did as he ordered. It's something anyway, she thought, as she raced about the church, closing doors, checking windows.

The south rear window of the sanctuary was open and, as usual, stuck. *"Not now,"* she muttered, slamming it with her fist. *"Oh, not now!"* It gave way and came down with a thud. For a moment she stared out the window, watching the man with the garden hose wet the elm tree and the clipped dry grass of the lawn.

His shoulder muscles moved in fluid rhythm beneath his soot-streaked shirt, and recognition dawned on Amanda. The harmony and the strength were there. And at the moment hard determination etched the man's stance, as if he felt the same as Amanda. He wasn't about to let the fire take anything he could possibly prevent. It was a fight, a challenge he intended to win. But the stream of water from the garden hose looked pitifully small against the flames growing ever closer, engulfing the fence.

Chapter Two

The churchyard was filled with vehicles and people milling in small groups, talking quietly of all they had seen and heard. Some, exhausted, sat on the steps, on the back of trucks or on the ground.

Amanda stood staring at the charred ruins and slowly peeled off the gloves Mae had given her approximately two hours and fifteen minutes earlier. In that time the fire had burned three-fourths of prime pasture, five acres of trees—some still burning—plus scrub oak that bordered the fences, Hammond's hay barn—also still burning—and the south wing of the church.

A sudden change of wind out of the north, turning the fire back upon itself, had finally brought about its demise. And a second fire truck had joined Old Red in extinguishing the remaining sparks and keeping the whole of the church from ruin.

Watching the firemen poke around the remaining charred frame of the south wing, Amanda felt extreme relief and thankfulness. The old building still stood. It was tough, seemingly invincible. That was comforting somehow. It could be repaired, the grass and trees would grow again, and no one had been seriously injured.

A crooked smile touched her lips. She'd not even thought of trying to save any one thing from the church—she'd wanted it all. It was amazing how she'd come to love the building, the whole rural area in fact, in only nine short months. After she'd traveled half the globe, it was as if she'd found her home at last in this small splotch on the map of central Oklahoma.

Slowly she turned and walked toward the north wing and the kitchen there. For the first time she was conscious of a strained ankle, aching muscles and chapped raw skin. She blinked and blinked again, for her eyes felt dry as yesterday's toast. People nodded and spoke.

"Bad bit of business, Amanda. Might start up again." This from Todd Walker, a pessimist in love with tragedy.

"You fought like a hellcat, Amanda!" John Tidwell called out across the yard, the offhand compliment as blunt and honest as the man himself.

"Praise the Lord!" Glenda Boyer shouted. Her overdone piousness generally got on Amanda's nerves, but tonight Amanda was too tired to feel annoyed, too tired to do more than smile and nod.

Light shone from the church's kitchen windows and two men, nodding politely, came out as she went in. Blinking in the bright light, she looked across the room to see a man bending over the sink, bare from the waist up, washing his face and tossing water over his thick hair. She recognized him immediately. The set of his back even bent over and his brown hair, showing auburn tints in the kitchen light, were almost intimately familiar.

Her gaze moved over his tanned back and lingered ever so slightly, then she stepped closer and reached into the cabinet for a glass.

Shutting off the water, the man straightened, beads of moisture sparkling in his hair and beard. Amanda handed him the nearby towel, at the last second noticing it was already streaked black from use.

"Oh...let me get you a clean one." She started to jerk back the towel, but his large hand gripped it firmly, his fingers brushing hers as he took it.

"This'll do. Just trying to clean out my eyes so I can see my way home." He spoke quietly, his voice deep and gravelly. And looking into his dark brown eyes, Amanda knew he was perhaps the strongest, gentlest man she had ever met. His eyes were large and round, the color of deep chocolate. Indian eyes, Spanish eyes. And they twinkled down at her, laughing even before the smile reached his lips. Then his teeth showed white against the dark softness of his beard. His deep chuckle came next.

"What is it?" Amanda asked, mystified.

"You sort of resemble a raccoon."

Instantly Amanda raised a hand to her cheek. Her fingertips came away sooty and she blushed. Tentatively she touched her hair, feeling the strands loosened from their braid, tangled and stiff. She looked down. Somewhere along the way, someone had given her a long-sleeved shirt to cover her own skimpier one. It was soot streaked and burned in several places, as were her once-white dress slacks.

"Here, let me..." Stepping closer, he dabbed gently at her cheek with the cloth. She watched his eyes, fascinated by their depth. Stopping, with the cloth in midair, he stared down at her, and in that instant Amanda felt herself being drawn toward him, though he didn't touch her at all.

Abruptly he dropped his arm and stepped back, breaking the strange spell. "I guess you'd better wash it yourself. Your skin is pretty red from the heat." He reached for his shirt.

"Thank you—for your help before," Amanda offered, wondering what in the world had happened between them and feeling suddenly very shy.

Cole nodded. "It's okay." He draped his shirt over his shoulder and strode quietly from the room.

Watching him, Amanda saw again the harmony of his body's movements. Almost absently she filled her glass, then leaned against the counter without touching her water. For heaven's sake, she thought. I'm attracted to the man. Then again, wonderingly, *For heaven's sake.*

It felt utterly delicious to fall into bed that night, the acrid smell of smoke scrubbed away. Every part of her body ached. For a long time she lay awake, watching lightning shoot across the sky and dreading the fact it could spark off another fire. But then the rain came. Better late than never, she thought, as it drummed on the roof. She had to laugh at herself. Here she'd been so worried about the church, and the parsonage across the street had been in danger as well. She'd never given it a thought.

Cole Mattox, for she thought that was the name she'd heard, came back repeatedly to her thoughts. As the fire had threatened the church, he seemed to be everywhere, directing others and joining in the battle where needed. It had been his order to Amanda to close all the doors and windows of the church that had saved the old building from complete destruction.

It was so odd, her reaction to him. Looking into his eyes, she felt as if she knew him, recognized him. Maybe it was a feeling of familiarity from having seen his truck several times. How silly, she thought, then played the feeling back through her thoughts.

The fire and all the excitement, that's all it is. She'd seen lots of handsome men in her life, hundreds, plenty of them bare chested and strong. After all, she had three brothers and they had friends.

He's not your brother, her mind whispered.

Just an overreaction to an attractive man, she countered. That's all. It will fade by tomorrow.

It was absurd, really and truly absurd. She'd left this sort of thing behind years ago. The choices she'd made through the years had put her farther and farther from that sort of relationship. It had passed her by. It was too late.

Amanda Jameson was thirty years old and deeply involved in her career. Thirty. Where had the years gone? Wasn't it just yesterday she'd planned out her life, sure that there was time for everything?—time to see the world, accomplish what she must, find the one man she dreamed of, have beautiful children and hear them call her Mama.

Where had the time gone?

She thought of the few men she'd had crushes on, and the one she believed she could have loved. What were they doing now?

Amanda sighed and looked up at the dark ceiling. Being a minister was rather like being a doctor: you were dedicated to healing and helping people and on call twenty-four hours a day—to everyone. Somehow your life got all wrapped up with the lives of others. There was little time to pursue your own social life or to make much of any personal life at all.

She'd always known this, of course. Her father had been a pastor, and her two oldest brothers had taken up the ministry as well.

Fully confident in her decision, Amanda had never questioned her reasons, even if the rest of the family and friends

thought her slightly bonkers. She still remembered the
morning she'd decided to enter the ministry. She was seven
at the time. She'd announced her intentions at the breakfast table and no one had paid her the slightest attention;
they'd all thought it was a phase. All except her mother,
who had buttered Amanda's toast and asked seriously,
"What about a husband and children?"

"Oh, I'll get married someday," Amanda had stated
confidently. "But I'm going to be a minister first."

She'd never changed her mind. Many times her mother
discussed it with her, asking the same question: "What
about a family, Amanda?"

Always Amanda had said, "Someday." There was a
world to see, things to do, people who needed her.

But someday just never seemed to come.

Until Paul. His image, blurred by time, came back to her
and she groaned inwardly. When finally she'd met a man
who'd been able to make her stop and think, it had been the
wrong time—for both of them.

She hadn't fully recognized the development of her relationship with Paul Venard during those first months she'd
been in Mexico. Or, perhaps more correctly, she hadn't admitted her feelings to herself.

Paul was a volunteer from France assisting several
churches in a hundred-mile radius and often stopped by to
spend a few days at the mission where Amanda was as-
signed. He and Amanda had taken to each other immediately. Paul was much older than she, a widower, terribly
handsome and lots of fun. He laughed heartily and argued
convincingly about everything, but in a good-natured way.
If any of the others at the mission noticed he and Amanda
seemed to pair off frequently, no one mentioned it.

And then one evening Paul took her hand. They were sitting outside enjoying the peaceful dusk of a day's end and

talking earnestly of the irrigation system Paul's corps and her own were working on along with the Mexican government. At least Amanda talked; Paul was unusually quiet, and watching him, Amanda fell quiet as well. For several weeks she'd been worried about him. He'd seemed easily distracted and irritable, not like Paul at all.

He took her hand and stroked it with his thumb. Amanda stared at his hand, feeling the roughness from hard manual work. And she knew, as if he'd transferred the knowledge by that small gesture. She swallowed, tears coming to her eyes. Somehow she also knew that any relationship between them would not bring joy.

"You know how I feel, Amanda," he said, looking at her steadily.

Unable to speak, Amanda only nodded.

"I waited until tonight to tell you. I'm leaving tomorrow morning." Amanda's eyes widened and she shook her head, starting to speak, but Paul touched her lips. "Shh...let me finish, *chérie*. It's not only the way I feel about you, Amanda. I...I think I'm in love with you, but I'm not sure. I'm all mixed up."

He paused a moment and Amanda waited. "A man of my age should not be all mixed up."

Again Amanda started to speak, then held her tongue.

"Fifteen years is not so great a difference between us...and yet, you have so much before you, I so much behind. Maybe it's not the years I feel, but that I know I'm not the man for you. I'm at a change in my life. I must finally figure out just who Paul Venard is." His voice was heavy and flat. Then he gave a sideways smile as he looked into the distance. "I gave my Laura a hard time when we were married. I don't want to do that to you, Amanda. And I loved her." The last he said as if he'd completely forgotten where he was and that it was Amanda he spoke to.

She tried hard now to remember the distinct image of his face, but all was blurred by time. Had she truly felt her heart breaking at that moment?

Paul had left the next day and Amanda had never had the chance to tell him how she felt about him. It would have been unfair that night. She couldn't bear to add to his burden. He'd only written once, two months later, to say he was fine, was working through a lot and that he knew he'd made the right decision.

That had been nearly two years ago. She'd missed him terribly and wondered what would have happened between them had they been in another time, another place. She pictured him, heard again his lilting French accent. She'd felt the beginnings of love for him. Would it have grown?

Sometimes, late at night, Amanda still wondered. It was at these times she recognized a seed of unrest within herself. It seemed to have been with her always. Perhaps this was what had kept her traveling, always looking to a new horizon. Something was missing within herself.

"It's time for you to go home, Amanda," Bishop Henderson had told her earlier when she'd still been in Mexico. "You're exhausted, you're not sleeping and you're wearing thin. What are you now? One hundred pounds?" Without waiting for a reply, he continued. "I've a letter from an old friend, Mae Loggin. I think you met her about a year ago when she toured the area."

Amanda remembered the woman: older, but one certainly wouldn't call her elderly. Amanda had expressed the need for writing paper and pencils for the children. A month later two large boxes had arrived, filled. A third box had contained books—brand-new ones, not castoffs. There was everything from beginning readers to collections of literature. All from Mae Loggin. No, Amanda had not forgotten the woman.

"You made quite an impression on her," Al Henderson said, "and she expressed a desire—if ever you could—for you to come to their church. It's old and small, sounds quiet and Mae says they need a young preacher." He chuckled. "I think she wants to stir things up. You'll be close to your family. And you'll have time to think—get to know yourself again. You're quite a beautiful woman, you know, Amanda," Al Henderson added with a smile.

Amanda had come and was glad. She enjoyed seeing more of her parents, who lived less than two hours away. And Coogan was a lovely place; it had a fine church with good people. They'd regarded her curiously, to say the least, but were equally friendly and inviting. And most had accepted her easily. Yes, she was a woman minister, not too common, but things were changing these days.

There had been a few raised eyebrows: Glenda Boyer thought it odd and not quite right. John Tidwell, male chauvinist that he was, was astounded, but he did give her a chance. The only total holdout was Pa Hammond, Roy's father. He was eighty years old and refused ever to accept Amanda as a bona fide minister. But he came every Sunday because, he said, she had a beautiful voice.

In Coogan, Amanda had her time to think, to find herself again. And for some unexplained reason, it was as if she'd come home.

Considering all this, Amanda decided she was being quite silly over her reaction to one Cole Mattox; it was a phase that would soon pass.

But something within whispered: *Is it?*

"Yes," Amanda said aloud and turned into her pillow. It was overreaction to the excitement of the night—overreaction to an attractive man; that was all. It would fade by tomorrow.

The fire brought quite a few changes into the lives of the people of Coogan. In some incomprehensible way, Roy Hammond and his eldest son had reached a reconciliation as they fought the blaze side by side, working together for the first time after four years of constant arguing and discord between stubborn father and willful son. Beth Doyle had her baby—one month overdue—and attributed it, gratefully, to the excitement. The insurance on the church was plenty, and a rather fancy new wing was being planned—the first improvement in twenty years. Glenda Boyer was feeling exalted at her high-blown self-appointment as interior decorator. Mae and Lowry Loggin, indeed several of the old-timers who'd run to help, were feeling new life and vitality. They'd been needed to show the youngsters what to do.

And for Amanda the fire had brought about the knowledge of the existence of one Cole Mattox. He'd rather blazed into her life, she thought with a wry chuckle. She'd found herself actually disappointed when she didn't see him at Sunday services. Wasn't he the least bit curious about her? Her eyes searched for his truck when she went to the grocery, though all the while she kept assuring herself her interest in him was a silly passing phase. And every time his image entered her mind, she shooed it away.

But thoughts of him didn't just disappear. They grew. It didn't matter how hard she told herself it was absurd, idiotic and just plain crazy.

The church resembled a wounded sea gull—one wing mangled, Amanda thought Monday morning as she strode quickly across the road separating the church from the parsonage. But it would soon soar again. Already, right after Sunday services, the men had begun tearing down the burned timbers in preparation for the rebuilding.

A smoky smell lingered, and Amanda threw up all the windows for fresh air. She didn't know if this would help much, though. The breeze from the south touched the burned pasture and brought the scorched scent with it.

She looked to the east, reveling in the sight of the glow of the rising sun and laughed fully, out loud. She was almost thankful for the fire. It had stirred her adrenalin, brought back into focus just how precious life is, how beautiful the world could be.

Or was it the fire? With a shake of her head, she dismissed the thought.

Since she was feeling especially feisty this morning, she decided it was the perfect time to deal with some long-overdue correspondence and the bills. The vast majority of churches had secretaries to deal with all of this, but smaller country churches like hers couldn't afford it. All the mundane, necessary paperwork was part of the job—and something she put off as long as possible. She flipped a coin to decide what to do first—bills won. For a moment, Amanda considered flipping again, but with a sigh, settled down to work. Soon her desk was cluttered with little piles: immediate payment, wait and inquire.

She was digging through the file cabinet when she heard the sound of a vehicle pulling into the churchyard. Her ears told her it was probably a pickup truck—the contemporary Oklahoman's horse. Pulling out a bulging file of canceled checks, she absently listened for someone to come in.

A minute later there came the sound of heavy footsteps treading cautiously. "Hello. Anyone around?" a low voice called out.

Instantly Amanda recognized the voice, her shoulders stiffened and she whirled toward the door. Surely it couldn't be.

But it was. The next moment Cole appeared in the doorway. He had a fresh showered look and wore faded denims and a deep blue T-shirt with the white image of a fifties' Chevy front end silk-screened across the chest.

"Well, hello," he said, his voice and expression betraying mild surprise, a slight smile touching his lips.

"Hello," Amanda replied, her eyes still upon him. It was happening again, a strange feeling of life surged through her. Involuntarily her hand went up to brush stray strands of hair into place. The thick file she held tilted awkwardly. Amanda tried to right it, but it fell to the floor, canceled checks spilling everywhere. She looked at the mess, unbelieving for a moment. Then she smiled at Cole. "Yes, good morning. Can I help you with something?"

He smiled in return, squatting to begin picking up checks. Amanda knelt beside him, feeling terribly clumsy. She could smell his enticing after-shave, and her senses vibrated at his nearness.

"I was looking for Lowry Loggin. I was supposed to meet him here this morning," Cole said.

"I haven't seen him." He handed her a pile of checks, and her eyes met his. "But you're welcome to wait. Would you like some coffee?" Amanda asked suddenly. It was the polite thing after all.

"Sounds good," Cole said, his voice rather slow and drawn.

She stuffed all the checks helter-skelter back into the file and placed it on the desk. "Have a seat. I'll only be a minute."

But Cole followed her to the kitchen instead. And she was conscious of his steps behind her every bit of the way.

"You don't in the least resemble that raccoon I saw Friday night," he said with an easy grin when she handed him his cup.

Amanda laughed. "I hope not."

"No lasting damage?" His perceptive gaze flowed over her face and slowly down her body.

"No." Quietly and unexpectedly pleased with the assessment, Amanda poured herself a cup and leaned against the counter. "Skin's a little tender, some scratches, but that's all. And thank you again. I guess I just froze when I saw all that fire around me. I sort of lost my bearings and couldn't figure out which way to go." Cole didn't reply, only sipped his coffee. "Which shocked you," Amanda asked, referring to that moment when she'd pulled the gunnysack from her head, "that I was a woman or that I was small?"

He glanced at her quickly, appraising her. He knew what she meant. "I guess both—maybe neither." He shrugged and Amanda saw something unrecognizable in his eyes. "Perhaps the fact that you weren't screaming your head off." Just when she'd decided that was all he was going to say, he spoke again. "It's a miracle this whole building didn't go up."

"Yes . . . yes it is."

He looked at her as if she'd said something funny. His grin was infectious and she grinned in return, noticing red highlights in his hair.

"You know, we've not really been formally introduced. My name's Amanda Jameson." With mock formality, she extended her hand.

"Pleased to know you, Amanda." He had a way of saying her name that made Amanda glad. He took her hand for a brief shake; his grip was rough and strong. "I'm Cole Mattox."

They both fell silent. Amanda sipped her coffee, then swirled it around in her cup. It reminded her of Cole's eyes.

"Have you fought many grass fires, Amanda?"

"A few—little tiny things, not like last night. I was born and raised up in the northern part of the state. We had our share."

"These fires can do a hell of a lot of damage in the right conditions," Cole commented, seemingly more to his coffee than to Amanda. "We were lucky the wind turned when it did."

"Oh, I don't believe in luck."

Cole regarded her a moment. "But you do believe in miracles."

"Yes," Amanda said slowly. "I suppose I do."

"I've not seen many." There was something beguiling in his voice, his manner, that drew Amanda's eyes to his.

"Perhaps you haven't looked." Amanda stared steadily at him, feeling the chemistry come alive between them. Did he seem to lean forward? Or was it she? His face was very close and Amanda held her breath, unable to move.

"No, maybe I haven't." His deep voice spoke the words scantly above a whisper.

His lips brushed hers, softly, fleetingly. They were warm and smooth, and his mustache tickled softly. Pulling back, he smiled. "Lowry just pulled up. Thank you for the coffee and conversation, Manda."

She stood stock-still as his work-roughened hand set the coffee cup on the cabinet. Then he quietly opened the kitchen door to the outside yard, stepped through and closed it just as quietly behind him.

She went to the window, careful to remain sheltered by the thin gingham curtain, and watched Cole walk over to greet Lowry. Wonderingly, she touched her fingers to her lips. He'd said Manda. Few people called her that.

As if drawn by a mysterious magnet, when Cole and Lowry walked around to the south side of the church,

Amanda ran into the sanctuary and knelt on the end of a pew to watch them through the window.

She watched the two men. Cole was pointing, Lowry nodding, as they faced the damaged south wing. What in the world were they talking about? Amanda, her conscience scolded, you should be ashamed. This is pure and simple eavesdropping. Still, Amanda watched and listened, trying to catch the men's words floating in snatches through the open window.

Cole said something about load factor and balance, Lowry about windows, but she couldn't catch all the words.

Then, like a slow awakening, Amanda's mind raced ahead. The burned-out wing . . . Lowry, who was on the finance committee of the church . . . Cole. Were they discussing the rebuilding? Would Cole do it?

She turned then and walked slowly back into her office, thoughts tumbling over themselves in her mind. Cole had kissed her. Well, could you truly call that a kiss? It'd been a simple brush of his lips. And with that motion, Cole had affected her as no other man ever had.

Why in the world had he done it? Well, he wasn't alone. She'd wanted him to kiss her. I hardly know the man, she told herself, and I wanted so much for him to kiss me, to touch me.

Was I that transparent? Amanda had never thought of herself as some lonely woman craving a man's touch. Her life had been too full for much loneliness to set in. What had Cole seen? Perhaps he thought it fun to play with the lady minister—give her something to think about. Her heart cringed at the degrading thought.

Again she came back to the fact that she hardly knew him. Odd how she didn't feel like that at all. When she gazed into his warm, brown eyes, she felt a definite kinship, almost as if she'd known him forever, an understanding that went way beyond words.

Yes, she was attracted to Cole Mattox. And deep within her heart Amanda knew it wasn't just a passing phase as others in her life. It wasn't going to just go away.

Hearing footsteps approach from down the hall, Amanda stiffened in her chair, not turning around.

"Morning, Amanda." Recognizing Lowry's voice, Amanda let out a low breath. She composed her face and sought to clear her mind. Even as the older man took the nearby chair, her ears picked up the sound of a truck leaving—Cole's truck.

"Hello, Lowry. Did Mr. Mattox find you?" She felt rather silly saying such a thing.

"Yep." Lowry paused. He was a quiet man, not given to saying one word more than was needed. "I wanted to get his opinion on rebuilding that south wing. We've enough insurance to handle the job—no sense waiting around. Besides, Mae's prodding my backside. Can you be up to the house for a finance committee meeting tonight?"

"Sure. What time?"

"Seven'll do."

"Tell Mae I'll come early to help with the refreshments," Amanda called after Lowry as he left.

A fresh westerly breeze blew through the window and touched her face. Amanda stared out at the field beyond, which was partially blackened now, not seeing. If Cole did the rebuilding, that meant he would be there most every day. Her mind ran over that thought several times, and she couldn't really figure out how she felt about it.

Chapter Three

Cole stared down at the sheet of paper on his drafting board, surprised to find his thoughts repeatedly returning to Amanda Jameson. When he'd first looked into her face that night of the fire, he'd thought he knew her. It was sort of like finding something he'd lost. He'd had the same sensation this morning. He remembered her eyes: a gold-green, wide and round. They flashed out from her face, revealing her emotions in a moment. And he remembered her brown hair, the color of light crystal honey.

He'd seen her before, tearing up the road in that red Jeep. And he'd wondered. Of course—he never missed a pretty face, he thought with a wry grin.

Cole wasn't quite sure what had gotten into him to make him kiss her. It just seemed the right thing to do, a natural happening. And those lips sure did invite a man, he thought, grinning again. They'd been warm and moist just as he'd imagined.

He brushed a hand across the paper as if to brush Amanda Jameson from his mind. He'd told Lowry he'd have some sort of estimate for him that afternoon, and he needed to get to work on the plans; they were simple enough.

But again his mind strayed. The name on the church sign read A. J. Jameson. A relative, obviously. Her father? An uncle? Why else would a woman like her be working as a secretary in a small country church? After all, there couldn't be that much to do. Maybe she only did it part-time, volunteering.

He supposed he could have asked Lowry, but he wasn't about to. Cole kept his feelings to himself. He'd find out more about her soon enough, he supposed. It might be pleasant working over there if she was going to be around.

Amanda habitually drove too fast, reveling in the heightened sense of freedom she experienced behind the wheel of her Jeep, its top down, the air blowing her hair. She whipped the flashy red vehicle from the blacktop and drove up the oak-shaded drive to the Loggins' home.

It was a typical farmhouse on the outside, appearing anything but typical inside. The furnishings were a combination Lowry, Mae and twenties' updated to eighties' style. It was warm, inviting and filled with pizzazz, as indeed Mae was herself, Amanda thought.

In her early twenties, and during a free-spirited youth, Mae had studied clothing design in Paris until the war and marriage to Lowry changed her plans. But the influence was still apparent. At seventy, a petite matriarch, Mae wore her steel-gray hair in a blunt bob and dressed with ageless style. And with a highly profitable ranch and producing oil wells, she and Lowry could well afford to live lavishly.

The older woman waved from the back porch as Amanda drove up. "You're going to get a ticket yet, Amanda. What will it look like when you tell the traffic judge you're a minister?"

Amanda shot her a grin.

"Just like me," Mae teased, and linked her arm through Amanda's as they walked up the steps. "Come on. Lowry's out feeding the cows, and we can have a nice chat before the others arrive."

Amanda was quiet, only half listening to Mae, as she spread cookies on a plate. She was mulling over a way to discreetly ask Mae about Cole—not wanting the older woman to get any foolish ideas—when Mae herself brought up his name.

"I saw no reason to look any further than Cole Mattox for a man to do the job," Mae said. "He lives close. We've known him since he was born. He called Lowry this afternoon with a very reasonable price."

"Is Cole a carpenter?" Amanda asked in a manner calculated to be offhand. "I mean, is that what he does for a living?"

"That, and ranching, like many others around here. He has about eighty acres—a section right across from the Hammond pasture that burned. That's why he fought so hard, afraid it could spread to his place. He runs some cattle and I hear is building himself a house." Mae poured them both glasses of iced tea.

That meant his ranch was just south of the parsonage itself. Something tickled Amanda's spine. "Funny how I've never met him with him living so close."

Mae shrugged. "No reason you should have, I suppose. He's only been home about six months, keeps to himself, though I understand he still has an eye for the ladies." Mae grinned wickedly. "He has since he was around eight."

"You sound as if you know him pretty well." Amanda didn't find this surprising. In an unobtrusive way, Mae Loggin knew a little about everyone and everything going on.

Mae thoughtfully sugared her tea. "Lowry and I were close friends with Ben and Dena Mattox, Cole's parents, but that was a long time ago. The Mattox family attended our church for years—just like everyone who lives around here. Then Ben got in a snit about something and started going over to Chickasha, and the Mattoxes have gone over there ever since."

She gave a bit of a chuckle. "That Cole—he was a rogue from the start, always into some sort of mischief. Then he went into the army and over to Vietnam for the later part of the war. He had some pretty tough experiences there and has had a hard time straightening out. He was hurt quite badly, his face scarred. That's why he came home for a while and then left. Ben told me Cole traveled around the country. Months would go by and they didn't know where he was. This went on for years. Then six months ago Cole came home again. He asked Ben for the part of the family land that would be his someday anyway, and Ben agreed."

"He's not married?" Amanda wished she'd bit back the question as soon as it left her lips. And somehow she felt sure he wasn't. She continued talking to cover her nervousness. "It seems rather odd. He looks to be maybe thirty-two or three. And handsome...I mean, surely plenty of women..." It was getting worse.

"No," Mae replied. "He's not married—never has been, as far as I know. And he's thirty-four. Yes, I'm sure he is because he was born the same year as our niece."

Both women fell quiet, Amanda picturing the warm gentleness in Cole's brown eyes and contrasting it with what

Mae had just told her. When she glanced up, she saw Mae's eyes on her, speculating.

"May I have some more tea?" Amanda asked, pointedly changing the subject.

There wasn't much to the finance committee meeting. Besides Mae and Lowry, there were only four other members, all old and close friends. In short order it was agreed the south wing of the church would be rebuilt exactly as it had been before, with the addition of double-paned windows and with heavy-duty wiring to safely handle larger loads of electricity. Cole would be in charge of the construction and handle the subcontracting of an electrician.

Amanda really wasn't sure why she was at the meeting, but she knew what was expected of her. Her seal of approval was more than a mere formality. As a minister, a lot was expected of her, and everyone had his own idea of what a minister should and shouldn't be, should and shouldn't do.

There were a dozen small instances. Glenda Boyer didn't think it right for Amanda to drive a sporty Jeep. More than four parishioners had nearly had heart attacks when, in an effort to interest young people in church, she'd organized teen dances on the parsonage's back patio. Several of the older members of the congregation thought she shouldn't wear jeans, and the younger teens thought the very fact she did made her easier to relate to. Todd Walker, who was single, took great pains never to be alone with her and was aghast to learn she liked modern rock as well as country music.

Amanda dealt with all this as tactfully as possible. She, and only she, could live her life, and not by a hundred other people's ideals and morals, but only by her own and what she believed God wanted of her.

Now Amanda found herself wondering what Cole thought of her. He had kissed her—not even knowing her—out of the blue. She could still feel the warmth of his lips. And the immediate heat of reaction from her own body. What in the world had gotten into her to act in such a way?

She wasn't sure she wanted to face Cole Mattox again. And yet, the anticipation refused to go away.

A cat smile touching her lips, Mae stood on the back porch, watching Amanda slip into her Jeep. The younger woman's hair caught the shine of the backyard light.

Amanda was interested in Cole Mattox; Mae was sure of it. They might have talked about every member of the church and everyone thereabouts, several single men even, but it was Cole Amanda wanted to hear about. It didn't surprise Mae at all. The two headstrong young people would be good for each other. And that was the reason Mae had insisted Cole be hired to repair the church.

"Well, I do what I can," she whispered.

Amanda worked on typing the church's weekly newsletter, ignoring the piercing buzz of the electric saw coming from the other side of the building. Cole had been working there for three days, and so far Amanda had succeeded in keeping out of his way. In fact, this was the first morning she and Cole had been at the church at the same time. She told herself that yes, though Cole was an attractive man, she had no intention of becoming in the least involved with him. There wasn't room in her life.

Why in the world would he be interested in her anyway? Surely he had his pick of young, desirable women.

Once that morning, however, she'd gone to the sanctuary and watched him through the window. He whistled while he worked, seeming to enjoy it, and his hands moved deftly.

Finished with the newsletter, Amanda covered the type-writer, gathered her purse and straightened her desk, preparing to leave. The Winfield Oil Company spared her their copier for running off the church newsletter every Wednesday at one o'clock.

When she tried to lower the office window, it refused to budge. "Oh, don't any of these old windows want to work?" she mumbled under her breath as she pulled with all her might. She stood back, leveling a rather hateful gaze at the stubborn window, but that didn't succeed in bringing it down either. For a moment she was tempted to leave it open, but a good wind could mess the office pretty well. Also, the heat was becoming sticky and she'd like to set the central air-conditioning unit to come on.

With a determined set to her mouth, Amanda found a hammer and pulled a straight-back chair from the corner. The chair wasn't quite enough, so she stacked first one book, then another, slipped her shoes off and climbed up. With the second smack of the hammer, the window gave about two inches and stopped.

"Damn!" Amanda whispered, then bit her lip.

The next second a low voice spoke from the doorway. "I do seem to find you in the oddest predicaments."

Jerking her head around at the voice, Amanda tottered and swayed. The books slipped and she would have fallen except with lightning strides Cole crossed the room and grabbed her hand, steadying her.

About the same time the hammer slipped and smashed one of the panes of glass on its way to the floor.

Looking at the window, Amanda let out a mournful sigh. Her gaze flowed downward, seeing the slivers of glass sprayed on the sill and around Cole's feet. Lifting her gaze from his feet to his eyes, Amanda felt irritation rise.

"I do wish you wouldn't sneak up on me." She shook her hand free.

His eyes had the nerve to twinkle. "Yep, I do manage to find you in the oddest positions." His gaze moved openly to her legs, encased in silky sheer stockings. "Mmm."

In unconscious reaction, Amanda raised one foot and rubbed it around her calf. With that movement she lost her balance again and was forced to grasp quickly for the window.

"I think you'd better come down from there." Then, without a pardon me ma'am, Cole placed his strong hands around her waist and lowered her to the floor.

For a long moment, Amanda found herself staring up into his brown eyes, her palms on his taut male shoulders for balance, while Cole smiled down at her, his hands lingering at her waist. She was intensely aware of the warmness from those hands, of his musky after-shave mixed with warm male scent, and of his twinkling eyes.

Agitated, Amanda stepped from his grasp and smoothed her dress.

"Well...thank you," she managed as she slipped her shoes on. She didn't feel thankful. She felt highly irritated and extremely self-conscious. Suddenly her dress, which was an expensive classic but purchased while she was still in college, felt terribly outdated and even dowdy. Every time she'd been around the man, she'd done something stupid. And he knew how she felt. She could see the knowledge in his laughing eyes.

That was enough, but to further her irritation, when Cole tugged at the window—with one hand—it came down smoothly.

Looking from the window to Cole, Amanda pursed her lips and walked out to find a broom and dustpan. When she came back, Cole was gone. Unaccountably, she felt disappointment tug at her. She listened for his footsteps in the hall as she swept up the glass. Moments later he returned with a square of cardboard and a roll of duct tape.

"This should hold it for a few days," he said, taping the cardboard over the hole. "I'll get a pane of glass the next time I drive into town."

"Thank you." Amanda meant it this time. It seemed she was always saying that to him. She dumped the glass into the wastebasket, and Cole finished taping the cardboard without further comment.

Amanda gathered up her things and waited politely to walk out with Cole. After all, I can't just rudely leave, she thought.

Turning, he said, "I found two Cokes in the kitchen refrigerator. If you keep quiet about my sneaking them, I'll share my lunch with you, Amanda."

Amanda smiled. "There's no need. No one will miss them."

"Have lunch with me anyway."

"No—I can't take your lunch." Amanda held up the typed sheets of paper. "Besides, I need to run this over to the Winfield Oil Company and have copies made."

And I have no intention of being around you any more than I have to, Amanda added silently to herself, not sure if it was Cole she didn't trust, or herself.

"You have to eat anyway. Share my lunch. I have plenty and I've already opened your Coke."

Amanda looked at him a minute. It appeared he was quite sure of himself—or else he didn't mind drinking two Cokes.... It was so tempting. She really wanted to.

As if reading her thoughts, Cole gave a slow smile. "Our place is reserved under the elms." He led the way to the kitchen, where, indeed, two small opened bottles of Coke sat on the counter.

They sat on the tailgate of Cole's pickup in the shade of several large elms. Amanda didn't fidget outwardly, but her blood seemed to race within her. Don't make such a big deal out of this, she told herself. For heaven's sake, it's just a lunch.

Yet she was distinctly aware of Cole's nearness, of his shiny hair just brushing his collar and of the way it curled over his ear. Today he wore a cream-colored T-shirt with the side view of a sports car printed in deep blue on the back. He must like fifties' cars, she thought, and I'll bet nostalgic rock 'n' roll. Very faintly she detected the warm smell of a manly after-shave.

There was a strong male sensuality about Cole, not something he himself was probably conscious of, but as much a part of him as his skin or the blood that pulsed through his body.

And somehow he made Amanda feel very aware of herself as a woman. Her skin tingled and the tips of her breasts hardened. A warmth, a pulsing which meant sublime life, started low in her stomach and ebbed and flowed throughout her body.

"You have a choice." Cole held out two sandwiches. "Peanut butter and jelly or peanut butter and jelly." His hands were the hands of a man who worked hard for a living.

"What a coincidence." Amanda laughed, reaching for one of the sandwiches. "You have my favorite. I could practically live on peanut butter."

"All of us who grow peanuts applaud you."

"You grow peanuts?"

"Not on my own place, but on the family land we do."

"Well, then—all of us who love peanut butter applaud your family."

"Thank you." Cole inclined his head magnanimously.

The breeze ruffled the leaves above, causing some to rain down on them. Amanda found herself looking at Cole. He simply looked back, not seeming to mind. After a second, he brushed a leaf from her shoulder. Vaguely unsettled, Amanda smiled slightly, then turned her gaze to the construction on the church.

"Where did you learn about building?" she asked. "Have you always done it?"

"Off and on. Growing up on a ranch, you learn the basics anyway. I got more training in the army. We built things— usually so they could be blown to pieces—then we built them again." Amanda detected a hint of raw emotion. "When I came home, I decided to make a living by it."

"You like it, don't you? I mean, you seem to enjoy your work."

"To me, it's like art. You take simple boards, two-by-fours, four-by-sixes, nails, insulation—things ugly by themselves—and you put them all together to form a building that not only pleases the eye, but shelters man as well. And it's a challenge to make it all come out right." He pointed to the main part of the church. "The middle part, the sanctuary, was built first. It's quite a bit older than the rest, but when the wings were added, they were done with care. See how the line is maintained?"

He bent closer, and Amanda felt his body warmth as she followed his finger with her eyes.

"I see what you mean. But how do you know that part is older? I mean, it all looks pretty old to me. I thought it was built in 1915."

"The main part was. The additions were made in 1948. I know because of the design of the eaves on the main section." Cole grinned. "Besides, my grandmother told me."

Amanda raised a teasing eyebrow. "Design of the eaves, huh?" Deep within her feminine heart, Amanda knew she was flirting with him—and he with her. It had sprung between them so naturally. It was a wonderfully new and thrilling feeling, one that made her feel off balance, dangerously so, but she was eager to experience it all the same. For a moment Amanda saw a totally different person in her reflection in Cole's eyes.

Their conversation remained light, almost nonsensical. Half an hour passed before Amanda even realized. Hastily glancing at her watch, she slipped to the ground, saying, "I have to go. They expect me over at Winfield before one."

In a fluid motion, Cole stepped down beside her. "Thank you for a most enjoyable lunch, Manda." His voice was low and lingered over her name. Amanda felt she'd never heard anyone say it with quite the inflection Cole gave it.

"You're welcome," she said, backing away. "... goodbye."

With her foot heavy on the accelerator, Amanda flew down the blacktop. She was rather disgusted with herself, acting like such an empty-headed child. Tom Winfield graciously lent the church his company's time and valuable copy machine each week and here she was allowing lunch with a man to make her late.

Lunch? Surely it wasn't truly lunch with a man. Not like a date or anything. Cole had simply shared his sandwiches and some pleasant conversation.

The description *pleasant* brought her up short. It had been pleasant, extremely so.

Okay, so she was attracted to the man. She could be honest about this. Any woman in her right mind—or out of it—

probably would be. It was a totally normal, very human response. It didn't mean all that much. In fact, it didn't mean a thing. She could enjoy Cole's company. What was wrong with that? She enjoyed Mae's company—and she enjoyed Lowry, Mary, Roy, and her group of teenagers from the church.... What was so strange about that? Nothing.

A chuckle began deep in her throat. Who was she kidding? Something happened when she was around Cole. Something magic and exquisitely wonderful. And she was glad. Perhaps her "someday" had come after all.

Cole watched Amanda slip gracefully behind the wheel of her Jeep, noticing again the smooth line of her leg. Winfield Oil Company. Apparently she did work part-time at the church, most probably for her father, and at Winfield as well. Watching the bright red vehicle disappear down the road, Cole was thoughtful. Lyle Winfield, Tom's brother, was a close friend of his, owed him ten dollars, in fact.

Late that afternoon, Cole dropped over to the Winfield offices looking for Lyle. He kept an eye out for Amanda as well, but didn't see her. Seated at the reception desk, Joanie Weeks smiled alluringly up at him. "Lyle's in his office."

Cole winked and went on through. "Come to collect my ten dollars from that bet on Friday night's race."

Lyle snapped his fingers. "Thought maybe you'd forget." He grinned broadly and reached for his wallet. "You going to the raceway again Friday night? There's going to be a special show of dirt bikes."

Cole dropped into a chair. "No...."

"Got a date, huh? Bet a lot of women are glad you finally came home, Cole," Lyle teased.

Cole shrugged and let it pass. "Tell me...is it some kind of rule you guys have over here—all your women employees have to be good-looking?"

Lyle grinned. "I tried that, but Dolly, Tom's secretary, wouldn't let me get away with it. I don't think my wife would either."

"Well, Amanda Jameson sure fits the bill. When did she start here? You've been holding out on me, friend."

Lyle just looked at him for a moment, and Cole wondered what was wrong. Then Lyle gave a half smile. "So you've met Amanda," he said slowly. "You must be slipping, Cole. She's been around here for about eight or nine months."

Cole shrugged and smiled. "So I've been busy. I'm taking time now, though. Is she related to the Jameson that's pastor over at the Coogan church?"

Lyle gave Cole a searching look and Cole wondered if Lyle himself might have a bit of a crush on Amanda. Then Lyle shifted his eyes, playing with a piece of paper on his desk. "Yes...yes, she is. Her father. And she's a nice woman. Real nice. And efficient. Amanda's real efficient. She handles our copying, some filing, stuff like that. Amanda's pretty standoffish, though. I'll bet even you couldn't make time with her...say, this ten bucks." His eyes twinkled daringly as he pulled a bill from his pocket. "And I'll give you a hint. I understand she loves soft music."

"I can't take your money again, Lyle, but thanks for the hint." Cole laughed and rose to leave. "Be seeing you."

Lyle Winfield watched Cole smile at Joanie as he left. Then he allowed his laughter to fully erupt. So Cole was interested in Amanda Jameson. And Cole didn't know! He really didn't know! Lyle had grown up with Cole Mattox and it seemed he and Cole had always been in competition. The best of friends, they were the best of rivals. And now all the jokes Cole had played on him over the years were finally coming home to his own doorstep.

Joanie brought some papers to his desk and looked at him quizzically. Lyle didn't say anything, just kept on chuckling. He hoped no one told Cole. And he wished he could be there when Cole found out he'd been having carnal thoughts about a preacher. A twinge of guilt touched him. Amanda was a nice woman. Lyle himself enjoyed looking at her, and she had a great sense of humor. He shrugged. Like as not she'd think it was pretty funny too.

It was ten o'clock at night, and restless, Amanda had grabbed her keys and driven to the Coogan Grocery for something extra sweet and gooey before they closed. She waited impatiently while Mrs. Anderson counted out her change. Normally she would have chatted with the friendly woman, but tonight she didn't feel like it. Her feet hurt, her head hurt, it was hot and she generally felt out of sorts.

"Allergies bothering you?" Mrs. Anderson asked sympathetically.

Amanda smiled wanly. "Seems like it, I guess. Thank you." She opened the door and the bell jingled.

"Take care," Mrs. Anderson called after her.

She backed the Jeep from its parking place around the side of the building and pulled up to the blacktop. Her eyes lit on Cole's truck parked a few yards down in front of the café. Involuntarily she felt her curiosity rise.

Though she'd tried to curb it, she'd found herself keeping a lookout for his truck everywhere she'd driven in the past week. Why? Why am I doing this? she kept asking herself.

She'd seen him several times since they'd shared lunch. She'd been in her office when he'd come to repair the broken window and two other times she'd thought up reasons to go to the church. Thought them up, mind you! She'd learned Cole did indeed like nostalgic rock 'n' roll: the

Beach Boys, the Everly Brothers, Buddy Holly. He was a walking encyclopedia about makes of automobiles. And they shared a passion for mystery books and coconut macaroons. Amanda laughed at herself. She was experiencing totally new and extraordinary feelings, and it was wonderful.

She was about to push on the accelerator when Cole emerged from the café with a woman hanging on his arm. Amanda sat riveted to the spot and watched.

The woman—girl, Amanda corrected—was quite pretty, with fluffy blond curls to her shoulders, a slinky dress showing off a streamlined figure, and three-inch spike heels. The girl smiled, leaning on Cole. Smiling back, he opened the driver's side of the truck and assisted her in. The girl turned and wound her arms around his neck and they kissed.

Irritation boiled within Amanda. She stepped on the gas, pulled out onto the highway, shifted into higher gear, and kept her eyes deliberately on the road.

Instead of pulling into her own driveway, she drove on and into the churchyard. The Jeep's headlights starkly illuminated the newly constructed framework walls of the south wing. Amanda wished she had the Jeep doors on so she could slam one. Stomping to the ground was unsatisfactory.

Gratefully she felt the peace of the church envelop her as she entered the sanctuary. Unlocking the door to her office, she switched on the desk lamp and sat quietly in its dim light, munching on the sinfully rich cake she'd bought and allowing herself to calm down.

What in the world was wrong with her anyway? She felt such a lack of something. Somehow, seeing Cole and that pretty woman simply pointed out the lack in her own life.

Very quietly she realized she wished she'd been that woman.

What an absurd notion, she mused. Cole was nice, handsome even, but they really didn't have anything in common. Especially if that was the kind of woman who interested him. She looked down at her own body. She wore a plain blue T-shirt and denim jeans. Well, she did fill out the slim-fitting shirt nicely, she thought with a jut of her chin. Her shoulders sagged. Somehow she felt reasonably certain her small sturdy frame wouldn't look the way the blonde's did in a slinky jersey. And she'd never owned a pair of spike heels in her life. They'd always seemed so useless.

With a dispirited sigh, she looked around the office. Since she couldn't sleep anyway, she might as well work. There was a bit of correspondence to deal with and her sermon as well as a paper on Anna Howard Shaw she'd been working on. Once into her research, she lost all track of time.

Suddenly she heard a noise from the sanctuary. At least it seemed to come from there. Amanda froze, listening intently, seeing clearly in that moment what she'd not thought of before. *There in the church she was isolated, alone, too far for anyone to hear her call.*

Chapter Four

Amanda listened intently. It was footsteps she heard. She was sure now. And they were coming closer.

There's the telephone, silly, she thought. But no; there wasn't time.

Quickly, with one part of her mind urging caution, the other prodding her imagination, she glanced around the room for something to defend herself with, her mind discounting possibilities in a flash. The typewriter was too heavy. Be serious, for heaven's sake! The letter opener was too messy—she couldn't imagine stabbing anyone. The paperweight! The old-fashioned glass—but it was too late to reach for it. The footsteps were nearly there.

Tightly gripping a book in her hand, she raised it over her head and stepped slightly behind the door, holding her breath.

A rap sounded on the doorframe. "Amanda?"

The next instant, Amanda was looking up at Cole, her face growing hot. *He'd done it again!* He'd found her in the most stupidly embarrassing position. How did this keep happening? She was an intelligent, totally reasonable woman. Why was it that whenever Cole Mattox happened on the scene, she appeared totally inept?

"Were you going to clobber someone or read them to death?" A grin tugged at the corners of his mouth.

Amanda let out a slow breath and lowered the book, thinking vehemently, if he laughs, I'll certainly clobber him.

"Must you always sneak up on me!" she said, plopping the book on her desk.

"I didn't sneak," Cole protested. "I drove by, saw your Jeep and the light and pulled in. Didn't you hear the truck?"

"No," she told him shortly. "I was busy."

"But you heard my footsteps?"

She shrugged. It certainly didn't make sense, but she wasn't going to admit it.

"Do you have so much to do that you have to work this late?" Cole asked, looking around.

"It's quiet here at this time. Not usually any interruptions."

"You shouldn't be here late like this, alone. Anyone could walk in."

"I know—they just did," Amanda said, as she busied herself gathering the books spread across her desk. She found it hard to remember she was a trained professional minister around this man, that she should remain polite and loving in manner. At the thought of the word *loving*, she mentally turned away. "I'm fine, Cole. Thank you for looking in." Her tone was ultrapolite. With short, precise steps she walked to the tall bookcase, replacing several books. One she had to stand on tiptoe to slide into place.

"Here, I'll get it," Cole said, attempting to slip the book from her hand.

"I can do it."

With pressure from both their fingers, the book slid into place. Amanda turned, intent on telling Cole to leave. Her head came to his shoulder, and she looked up into his intense dark eyes. It was as if a magnet drew them together, and Amanda felt her breath catch in the back of her throat.

His arms came around her, enveloping her into the heat of his body, and she watched his lips until she could only feel them against her own.

A kaleidoscope of impressions bombarded Amanda: the firmness of the chest against which she pushed, the scent of after-shave mixed with that of warm skin, and the overwhelming strength of the arms that held her.

At first she tensed her body and struggled to push away. Still holding her tightly, Cole drew back and his heavy-lidded eyes fastened on hers, questioning. All she could do was look into their warm cocoa depths. Their light softened, drawing Amanda into their magic. Then one strong hand tenderly moved to the back of her neck, massaging into her hair and sensitive skin. His warm lips again moved over her own, claiming them with a gentle but determined pressure. By instinct, Amanda parted her lips, welcoming him, giving to him in return.

His tongue flitted over her own and a glowing warmth enveloped her body, starting from her stomach and flowing throughout her limbs. It was a wonderful, delightful feeling. Her legs gave way as she instinctively relaxed against Cole, feeling the warmth, the strength of his frame. Tentatively her hands inched from his chest and wrapped around his sides, feeling his body beneath the soft cotton of his shirt. Her being spun away into a timeless realm comprising only sensations—exquisite sensations. She experienced them all with a sense of wonder. She was an explorer, eager to learn, yet cautious too.

Cole's rough hands moved gently to cradle her cheeks as he pulled his head away. Their bodies remained touching; his eyes were on hers. He stroked her skin with his thumbs while Amanda stared at him, mesmerized. She blinked, struggling to bring herself back to the moment. Her breath came fast as her heart pounded in her ears. A coolness touched her burning cheeks.

What was she doing? How? Why? Confused thoughts tumbled over one another: embarrassment, wonder, shock, all rolled up together. Cold shivers flowed over the warmth she had experienced before.

And Cole's eyes still looked at her questioningly.

Amanda pushed at his chest, and he let her go. She turned toward the desk, unable to look him in the face any longer. She didn't have any answers. She wasn't even sure of the questions. She just knew she had feelings that threatened to overtake her, feelings she shouldn't have for a man she hardly knew, had just met. Should she? And only this evening she'd seen him in the arms of another woman.

She didn't understand herself at all. Not at all.

Rubbing a hand through his hair, Cole took a deep breath. He didn't know if he'd offended her and wasn't quite sure what to say or do. Hell, he didn't even know what was going on. Just that there was something between them, something alive and electric. There had been since that first night he'd sat on the hard ground and found a little bundle of energy with luminescent eyes staring up at him.

And she'd seemed so familiar.

And that had just been one hell of a kiss.

Well, he'd better say something, he decided, still uncertain as to quite what it should be. But you couldn't just kiss a woman you hardly knew—like that—and let it go.

"I didn't mean to—" He stopped. He wasn't going to apologize for the kiss. He'd liked it and was reasonably sure she had too. Okay. So now what? She could very well stand there rigid as stone all night.

She turned her head slightly, and he could see the curve of her silken cheek. "Do you make a habit of this? Grabbing woman and kissing them? I mean, is it some sort of hobby?"

"Not generally. Do you want an apology? I kind of got the idea you enjoyed it." He was on the verge of a chuckle, but held it in. "I know I did."

She turned toward him, her face a pale mask, though her green eyes reflected a question.

"I think I'd better go home now," she said.

Still Cole felt he should say something, but didn't know what. He waited by the door as she picked up a couple of books and her purse. She closed and locked the office door and they walked through the short hall and shadowy sanctuary, lit only by reflection from the floodlight outside. Neither of them said anything; tension crackled between them.

On the porch, Amanda turned to check the double doors. "They don't quite catch sometimes."

"Aren't you going to lock them?"

Amanda shook her head. "No. If anyone needs in, the church is open and waiting for them. I only lock the office because the checks and sometimes money are kept there. But if anyone really wanted in, they could manage easily."

Cole walked her to the Jeep and put his hand against the roll bar. "Amanda..." He paused to straighten the words in his head—and to make sure he wanted to say them. "Would you like to go to dinner tomorrow night? Christopher's, in the city?"

It seemed like forever before she answered. "Yes. I'd like that very much." A slight smile curved her lips. She started the engine and shifted into gear.

Cole stepped back and watched her lights disappear from the churchyard, then reappear across the street at the parsonage. Then he got into his truck and drove away.

Back in his small trailer, Cole pulled a beer from the refrigerator, popped the top and walked outside. The night was warm and balmy; coyotes called in the pasture beyond.

He was nervous about what he'd just done. He liked Amanda, liked her a lot. It had been a long time since he'd had feelings like this, since he'd even allowed himself to believe he could feel again. He'd screwed up his life pretty well even before Vietnam and the war had done more damage. Since then he'd spent the better part of ten years trying to straighten out.

He'd been trying hard this past year to get his life in some sort of order. After all, he wasn't getting any younger, and he really did want a wife and family. He grinned. He still was playing around too much with too many women. It was just that he hadn't found that one, that special one.

The memory of Amanda's lips lingered, and he remembered the banked fire he'd sensed within her warm trembling body. He'd never met a woman like her, and wasn't quite sure about getting involved with her. And to complicate matters, he had the disquieting feeling he was already involved, had been the moment she'd fallen into his lap.

Quit blowing it all out of proportion, he ragged himself. All he'd done was ask a pretty woman out for the evening. They'd have a good time. He grinned in the darkness. Lyle Winfield's pride would sure be sore.

He went to bed thinking of it all. At one-thirty he realized he hadn't told Amanda what time.

Amanda didn't think she'd ever sleep. She kept trying to understand herself and her reaction to Cole. How could she have kissed him like that? For heaven's sake, she hardly knew him! And she'd wanted to do it again! She'd almost walked into his arms again simply to find out if it would be the same.

She tried to pull her emotions out one by one, as if to spread them upon the sheet and examine them, but she kept getting all confused. Finally she fell into a fitful sleep.

She awoke late and surprisingly refreshed. It was as if her subconscious had put many of the pieces together. She was attracted to Cole. No denying it. And he was attracted to her—how much, she didn't know, but he was. She knew that for certain. She wanted to go out with him tonight; she wanted to be with him.

Half whistling and half singing, Amanda showered and dressed. A picture of the young woman she'd seen with Cole floated across her mind. She'd have to do some shopping—definitely.

She ended up driving all the way into Oklahoma City, to the south side and a large shopping mall there. At the third store she tried, an exclusive one she remembered from school days, she found a beautiful eggshell knit dress accented with a narrow gold belt. The dress's draping neckline complemented her face, and the kitten-soft fabric flowed over her frame.

Amanda stared at her reflection in the mirror. Somewhere between high school and now, mixed in with all the years she'd had her nose in books and her body in hard physical work, she'd become a full-fledged woman. Rather surprised, but thoroughly pleased, Amanda ended up purchasing a linen skirt, a matching blouse and two pairs of trousers. At the last minute she spied a lovely blue nightgown with a matching robe and added this to the pile. The clothes were all expensive, but timeless in design and craftsmanship. They would last for years.

"You have the look of a woman in love," the saleswoman commented.

Amanda looked at her and blinked, then smiled self-consciously. She's imagining it, she told herself. I'm just...well... She didn't know. "I guess it's the weather—it's beautiful outside."

On her way out of the mall, she stopped in front of the wide windows of a shoe store and looked uncertainly at the spike heels. Then her eyes lit on just the sandals for her. Fifteen minutes later she had them beneath her arm and was thanking both God and her grandfather, who'd been wise enough to get in on the ground floor of the oil business and who'd passed on trust funds to Jameson heirs.

At home, she spread her purchases on the bed, admiring them once more. The telephone rang.

"Amanda Jameson."

"Reverend Jameson, this is Steven Tidwell. I'd like...well, I need to see you...about getting married today."

Amanda knew Steven. He was the youngest of John Tidwell's sons. Until recently he had been away in college. At the moment he sounded terribly nervous and this was the first she'd heard of any marriage plans.

"Suppose I meet you at the church office in...fifteen minutes. Is that soon enough?"

"Yes ma'am!" His tone now reflected his eager excitement.

Amanda walked across to the church. Cole was measuring two-by-fours under the shade of an elm. Catching sight of her, he waved and Amanda waved back. Her heart skipped several beats as her gaze took in the familiar harmony in his movements. Automatically she brushed stray wisps of hair from her forehead.

Barely five minutes later, footsteps sounded softly through the sanctuary and down the hall. Steven entered, holding the hand of a young girl. That they were so young was Amanda's first impression, as scattered worries forced their way into her thoughts. Firmly she cleared her mind and smiled invitingly at the young couple.

"Reverend Jameson, this is Marcy Andrews," Steven said. The young girl smiled hesitantly, clinging with all her might to Steven's hand. "We'd like to get married." He held out a folded sheet of paper. "We have the license."

"Hello, Marcy." Amanda gave her a warm smile. She vaguely remembered Steven bringing her to church several times in the past months. "Please call me Amanda—you have before, Steven," she reminded him. Taking the license, she noticed Steven's hand quiver and saw the uncertain light in his eyes. She gestured to the leather chair beside her desk and pulled another over beside it. "Suppose you both sit and tell me the situation. I assume there is some reason your parents aren't here—perhaps don't even know?"

"Oh, we don't have to get married," Marcy said hurriedly. She was a pretty girl—eighteen, Amanda saw on the license. Steven was nineteen.

"We want to get married," Steven stated in a stubborn tone. "And we're not going to change our minds." He sat with Marcy's hand in his own. "You might as well know, my parents are against it. They want us to wait. But I love Marcy and we want to be married now."

"What about your parents, Marcy?" Amanda asked gently.

"There's just my mother. She lives up in Tulsa. We're not very close."

Amanda sat quietly looking from one to the other. What now? She could well imagine John and Leeann Tidwell's reaction. John wasn't known for an even temper. They wanted their youngest to be a doctor. Steven was in his second year at college.

"How long have you two known each other?" Amanda asked.

"A year and a half," Steven answered evenly. "We don't want to go to a justice to be married, Amanda. I thought . . . well . . ."

Amanda silenced him with a flutter of her hand. She got up and walked to the window, thinking of all the things she could say and discarding them. The two were set. There was nothing she could tell them that they probably hadn't considered. Yes, they were young, but Amanda herself had barely been eighteen when she'd entered college firmly intent on the ministry.

Sighing, she reached for her purse. "As my wedding gift, I would like to give you the weekend at the Park Suite Hotel. I'll call and arrange it. And here." Amanda pulled several bills from her wallet. "Have a honeymoon dinner on me."

Steven shook his head, his jaw taut.

"Please, Steven. Is it polite to refuse a gift?"

The young man grinned slowly. "Thanks."

"Marcy, you go freshen up," Amanda ordered, reaching for the telephone. "You too, Steven. I'll get us some witnesses."

She dialed Mae Loggin. "We're to have a wedding, and I need a witness. And bring some flowers and rice," she told the older woman.

Then she looked up the number and dialed the Park Suite Hotel, reserving a room for the young couple on her charge card. With the clothes she'd bought earlier—also on charge—Amanda had blown five months' allowance in one day. Her grandfather would have something to say when he received the bills. But the kids needed a good start. One could never tell. A nice honeymoon could just make a difference. Amanda sighed. She still needed another witness.

Cole cut the saw, lifted his safety glasses and looked up, a slow smile spreading across his face.

"Can you get cleaned up a bit?" Even with her thoughts on Steven and Marcy, she noticed how handsome Cole was and felt herself reacting to that smile of his. "We're going to have a wedding, and we need a witness."

"A wedding?" Cole looked bewildered.

"Yes. You've heard of them, haven't you?" She chuckled and stepped away, urging, "Come on, get moving. The kids are in a hurry." She fairly skipped back into the sanctuary. It was a beautiful day for a wedding. How exciting! She had to find her wedding-ceremony stole and comb her hair.

Mae arrived, greeted Marcy warmly and handed her a lovely bouquet of fresh flowers, complete with ribbon and lace. Aside she said to Amanda, "You know John's not going to be too happy."

"I'll deal with him later," Amanda whispered, her mind racing ahead, checking every detail. Though the wedding would be a small affair, she wanted it to be beautiful for Steven and Marcy. Amanda hoped it would be the only one they would have, a cherished memory.

The afternoon sunlight lit the sanctuary. The young couple stood at the front of the church holding hands and smiling at each other. Mae began soft organ music. Occupied with adjusting her silk stole so its fringed ends hung even, Amanda bumped into Cole in the hall.

With his hands on her upper arms, he smiled down at her. "Looks like everyone's ready and waiting. Where's the preacher?"

"Oh, I'll be there in a second," she said gaily. "I'm just going for my Bible...." But the look on Cole's face stopped her, and her last words trailed off. His smile froze and then slipped away altogether, replaced by a look of total shock. His gaze moved from her face and lit on the ceremonial stole, then back to her eyes, registering confusion and disbelief.

Amanda found she couldn't move away from him or take her eyes from his. She watched as his brown eyes darkened. The blood pounded in her ears. They stood facing each other in the dimness of the hallway, the moment suspended in time. Amanda could neither blink nor catch a breath. And in that moment she could read his thoughts.

Why hadn't she realized?

She'd simply never given it a thought, had taken for granted that he knew who she was.

But he hadn't.

She saw that now.

"You didn't know," she stated, her voice low. With his eyebrows drawn together, Cole's gaze searched her face, then again flowed downward, taking in the white silk stole. How in the world had it happened? Amanda thought. *How had he not known?*

Gingerly she touched Cole's shirt, and he dropped his hands from her arms. He didn't say anything. Dimly the organ music floated to Amanda's ears. Her brain reminded her there were two young people waiting for her—and for a most important event in their lives. Amanda stepped away. She would have to deal with this later.

When she reached her desk, she picked up her Bible and flipped through it to find the passages she wished to read. For a moment she gripped the desk. *How had this mix-up happened?* She'd been here at the church, and surely he'd talked to other people in Coogan or had seen her name on the sign out front.

Firmly she put the thoughts aside. This moment belonged to Steven and Marcy. She must give them all her attention.

Taking her place facing the young couple at the altar, she looked from one to the other and gently smiled. Steven's face was earnest, Marcy's exceedingly pale. For the briefest of seconds, Amanda's gaze strayed to Cole who was standing well behind them. His face was impassive now. Mae's organ music trailed off, and Amanda began, "Steven...Marcy. We are gathered here to unite you together as man and wife...."

"Love suffers long and is kind..." Amanda read just after formally pronouncing the young couple man and wife. There came the roar of a car driving into the churchyard. Amanda tensed, feeling the hairs on the back of her neck stand on end, but she continued, "Love does not envy...."

A car door slammed. Seconds later John Tidwell burst through the doors of the sanctuary and stalked down the aisle. Leeann came behind him. It was uncertain whether she was backing him up or trying to stop him. The five of them at the front turned and stared. Marcy sort of melted into the protection of Steven's arm, while Amanda stepped forward to face John.

"Stop it!" John's voice boomed. "Stop it right now!" A big man, he resembled a raging bull at the moment. Leeann put a hand on his arm, but he shook it away. He hitched up his pants and stood with one hand on his hip, glaring first at Steven and Marcy and then focusing on Amanda. She felt exceedingly small before him, but not intimidated. Brushing a hand across her forehead, she faced him squarely.

"Belle Peters from over at the courthouse called us. I couldn't believe it! What in the hell do you think you're doing?" John hollered. He jabbed at the air in Steven's direction. "That's my boy and I told him he could not marry this girl. I won't have it—not the likes of her!"

Steven erupted, pushing Marcy aside. "She's my wife now. You can't talk like that!" He flung himself at his father, and all Amanda could think to do was throw herself between them.

She vaguely heard Cole call, "Amanda, get out of there!"

Steven and John grappled around her, and she felt herself squished by their bodies even as she tried to force them apart, pleading for peace. Someone tugged at her hand and heavy male feet stamped on her own.

Feminine voices shouted, and Cole's deep voice penetrated the melee as he drew John away. "Stop it, John!" He struggled with the big man while Amanda and the other women tried to restrain Steven. "That's Amanda you're about to hit."

John twisted in Cole's grip. "I should! Damn you, Amanda! If you were a man, reverend or no reverend, I'd bust you in the mouth!"

Everyone started yelling at once and Amanda again pleaded for reason, first with one, then another, but no one paid her the slightest bit of attention. Then somehow Steven and John were at it again, Cole in the middle this time. John managed to free an arm and swung. Amanda doubted if he cared whom he hit; he just wanted to punch. John's huge fist made contact and Cole sprawled across the floor, landing near the altar.

"Oh, my..." Amanda knelt beside him, the others momentarily forgotten. The skin on his cheekbone beneath his left eye was broken. It oozed blood and was swelling rapidly. This was enough.

"Quiet!" Her voice echoed in the tall-ceilinged sanctuary, lingering as everyone froze and stared at her.

Self-consciously she smoothed her hair, which had fallen around her face. Glowering at her, John disengaged himself from Steven and the women and straightened his sleeves. Leeann looked worriedly from father to son, and Steven held tight to Marcy, who appeared close to tears. Mae seemed to be holding her breath. Cole's eyes twinkled and his lips threatened to break into a smile, though he was still sprawled on the floor, tenderly fingering his cheek. Amanda glared at him in warning. He'd better not laugh. He'd just better not!

"John," Amanda began, "I knew you didn't want Steven to marry. He told me honestly. But they came to me for a marriage with God's blessing. It's their right, John. Steven is nineteen years old. He's a man. And you would do well to remember he is your son and now Marcy is his wife." Again she repeated, "He is your son, John." She bent to pick up her Bible, which had been knocked under a pew. Deliberately she smoothed the pages, straightened her shoulders and stole and stepped back to her place on the altar stair. "Now, we have a ceremony to finish." Her tone brooked no nonsense.

John looked at her, his face still angry. Cole gingerly rose and stepped back behind Steven—who continued to hold Marcy—but faced Amanda, his expression determined. Mae gave a pleased cat-smile and nodded encouragingly, and Leeann forced her hand into her husband's.

Amanda finished reading the verses, feeling she was now aiming them at John. When she'd finished, Leeann stepped over to the young couple, looked at John and back again. Then she bent and kissed Marcy on the cheek. "Welcome to the family," she said softly but firmly.

Turning on his heel, John stalked out.

Cole's expression was unreadable, though he winced as Amanda dabbed a cold wet cloth against the broken flesh high on his cheekbone. The whole area surrounding his left eye was swollen blue and violet. Amanda's spirits sank lower, if that were possible. For a day that had started on a high note, it had certainly gone downhill.

"Ouch." Cole winced and pulled away.

Amanda handed him the cloth. "You'd better hold that against it for a few minutes to help with the swelling." Nervously she dried her hands, half turning from him. "I'm so sorry, Cole."

He gave a half grin. "Do you have many such weddings, Preacher?"

The way he said "Preacher" rather stood out. By some odd mix-up, he'd not known. But why did it matter? She was still Amanda Jameson, the woman he'd grabbed and kissed—twice.

But apparently it did matter—a whole lot.

Chapter Five

Ignoring the teasing question, Amanda asked in a low voice, "Who did you think I was?"

His expression guarded, Cole answered, "The secretary..." Amanda's eyes widened. "Well, every time I saw you, you were in the office typing or messing with the files. And Lowry said to give you the invoices and you'd write the checks. I figured you were the secretary or helper...or something. And what was all this business about going over to Winfield Oil? Lyle said—" He stopped.

"Lyle said what?"

"Nothing..."

Amanda stared at him a moment. "Tom Winfield lends us his copying machine. I go there Wednesdays, one o'clock, to run off our weekly newsletter. Our church is too small to have a secretary. It's my job to handle all the business details as well." Her voice was flat, her heart sinking lower by the moment. "Didn't you see my name on the sign in front?"

"A. J. Jameson," Cole said flatly.

Amanda winced inwardly. "Amanda Jean," she said, staring at him. "Well, who did you think A. J. was?"

"Your father, your uncle . . . somebody. I never gave it a great deal of thought. The assumption just formed in my mind. I figured A. J. Jameson was your father and you helped out at the church and worked over at Winfield Oil. . . . They employ quite a few women in their offices. Why else would a woman like you be living out here? You're not from here originally, and you did say you had to get over to Winfield that day."

"That's really assuming a great deal." Annoyance rose in Amanda. "What do you mean 'a woman like' me?"

Cole looked at her quietly for a moment. "You have to admit you certainly don't fit the minister mold."

"Oh?" Amanda's tone turned frosty and fell a shade lower. "Just what mold is that?"

"I don't know. . . ." Cole raked a hand through his thick hair and threw the wet cloth into the sink. "A person doesn't expect a minister to drive around in a flashy Jeep like yours, or to find them out beating at fires and falling into their laps—"

"Get to the point," Amanda interrupted. "It bothers you that I'm a woman minister."

Cole's eyebrows came together. "That's beside the point. . . ."

"Oh, I think that's the point entirely."

"I don't like having words put in my mouth, lady," Cole said, his gruff voice rising. "The point is, a person may be thrown for a moment by your sex . . . your . . ." He gestured at her, his eyes raking her up and down. "Anyway, no one expects to see a minister look like . . . and flitting around in that flashy Jeep, and . . ."

"That Jeep was a birthday gift from my brother," Amanda said, her words clipped. "He felt I needed something like that to get around to some of the out-of-the-way places out here. And I happen to like the cheerful color of red. What is a minister supposed to look like? A woman minister, to be precise?"

"I don't know precisely," Cole said hotly. "But a minister should listen and quit butting into a person's sentence. And you don't expect to find a minister climbing up onto books on chairs. And swearing—I heard you swear! Or hammering on windows or knowing more about construction than the average woman." His tone cooled. "And flirting—you were sure flirting with me that day we shared lunch. A man doesn't expect that from a minister. He doesn't expect a minister to end up with a brawl in the church—or for a minister to kiss him the way you kissed me!"

Cole pointed his finger at her, and she pointed right back at him.

"I'm sorry to disappoint your warped vision of women of God dressed in drab gray dresses, gray hair pulled back in buns and pinched old severe faces that never smile. I hate to tell you, but Mother Nature made some of us women foolish just so we could match you men. Some of us laugh and get a lot of joy out of life. And we know about such worldly things as cars and construction. And I'm a minister—not God! Sometimes I do slip up and swear. I can't govern where a brawl between a bunch of adolescent males is going to take place. And you kissed me!"

She was angry now. Thoroughly and totally furious. What with the problem with John and now this, she felt she'd been stomped on enough. Cole stood before her, and she was forced to tilt her head to look him in the face.

"And to further erode your outdated, egotistical, just plain stupid opinion of what a minister should be—my family happens to have money. If you haven't heard of Jameson Trucking, perhaps you've heard of Jameson Flanges?"

A warning sounded in the back of her mind as her temper reached eruption point. Realizing she'd been gesturing with both arms, she balled her fists and held them to her sides. In a very low, measured voice she said, "As for the flirting, I don't believe it's a sin for a single minister, either male or female, to be friendly with a member of the opposite sex." Then because she was too angry and embarrassed at her loss of control, as well as annoyed at the ring of truth in much of Cole's words, she said tightly, "Thank you for your assistance this afternoon. Good day, Mr. Mattox."

Turning, with her back rigid, she strode from the kitchen.

Cole hollered after her. "I may have kissed you, but you sure did some kissing back!"

Amanda refused to turn around, but kept on striding across the churchyard and over to the parsonage. Her shoes clicked loudly upon the porch. She realized she half hoped Cole would come after her. Throwing the thought away, she mentally stomped on it. A minute later she heard Cole's truck leave the churchyard.

The tears flowed then, coursing hotly down her cheeks. How could she have said all those things to him? How could she have acted so juvenile and so idiotic?

Oh, what a temper, she thought mournfully.

And that temper rose again. He'd made her feel outlandish, unprofessional and inept. He'd cast aspersions on her ability as a minister. What a ludicrous picture he painted just because she was a clergywoman. Amanda laughed through her tears.

What did it matter how she looked or what kind of vehicle she drove, as long as she got the job done? And who was going to shut the window that day? Could she help being short? Just because she was a clergywoman, she wasn't supposed to wield a hammer? Wasn't supposed to know anything?

But Cole'd been right about so much, she thought remorsefully. She had flirted with him, had kissed him and enjoyed it. But what in the world did he think? There surely wasn't anything wrong with that. And she'd had no idea he didn't know she was the minister. He acted as though she'd done something wrong on purpose. She hadn't deliberately tricked him, for heaven's sake.

Why should her being the minister make such a difference? The moment he'd found out, he'd looked at her as if she had horns—or perhaps wings and a halo would be more correct, certainly just as odd. He didn't see her anymore.

Amanda sighed. She had experienced this before. It made a great deal of difference to a great many men. Just as many men didn't care for a woman construction worker or a woman who managed to become a magnate in business.

Yes, she'd experienced it before, but it had never hurt, not like now.

And never would she have expected such asinine behavior from Cole Mattox. The very thought made her cry even harder. She was angry, confused, and above all, humiliated at her behavior. She should know better, should have better control of her emotions. After all, she was professionally trained.

Amanda sat and allowed the tears to flow until there were no more and she felt drained of emotion. When her gaze strayed to the clock and she saw it was nearly five, it dawned on her she was to have gone out with Cole tonight. Obviously that was off.

She wandered into the bedroom and stared down at the newly purchased clothes still lying on the bed. She fingered the eggshell knit dress. It was so pretty. For a moment, she pictured Cole. Amanda shook the thought aside. The date was off, she told herself firmly.

The shrill ringing of the telephone startled her. It rang two more times before Amanda could move and step across the room to answer it.

"I'll pick you up at six," Cole's voice came across the line gruffly.

Surprised, Amanda sucked in a breath.

"Okay?"

"Yes," Amanda managed. "Fine. You know where I live?"

"Yes," he said, and the dial tone sounded.

Amanda slowly replaced the receiver, and her hand rested on it briefly. "What a strange man," she whispered. He certainly was unpredictable. He didn't so much as ask her if she still wanted to go. No apology. Just words spit out practically like an order. What had prompted him to keep the date? she wondered. And what in the world had prompted her to say yes?

She couldn't very well have said no, she told herself. He was making an effort to be polite. It would have been rude to decline, even unforgiving.

Glancing at the clock, Amanda sped into motion, arguing with herself the whole time. Be honest, she scolded her reflection in the mirror. You want to wear that new dress and feel gorgeously feminine. And you want to see the inside of Christopher's. The outside looks classy. It had been years since she'd been to such a place.

And she wanted to see what Cole Mattox was like away from his work.

Tonight, she decided at last, should at the very least prove interesting.

She heard the truck, and from the shelter of the curtain watched him walk in long purposeful strides up the walk. He wore slacks, a slim-fitting sport shirt opened casually at the neck and a Western-style coat, all in varying shades of brown and tan—which suited him perfectly. Even in these more formal clothes, he exuded a rugged edge. Amanda felt herself strongly attracted, and it made her nervous. She wasn't sure how he expected her to act. She wasn't even sure how she expected herself to act.

Cole towered in the doorway when Amanda opened the door to his knock. Tension crackled between them. For a second she panicked and wondered what to say. He looked equally uncertain, and Amanda winced inwardly when she saw the small bandage to the side of his left eye. A blue-violet bruise spread above and below the bandage into the thickness of his hair and beard. Sinkingly Amanda recalled the afternoon's fiasco and her hot temper.

At her look, Cole touched his fingers to the wound. "It's not so bad—I've had worse."

Amanda backed up, allowing him to enter. "I'm really sorry about that, Cole." She took a breath. "And I'm truly sorry for losing my temper this afternoon. I said quite a few things . . . well, things I didn't mean exactly."

A smile threatened his lips. "Not exactly?"

"No—not exactly," Amanda repeated, growing irritated at his manner—which she didn't quite understand—and at her own as well. A strong, vibrant awareness pulsed between them, setting her nerves on edge.

"I apologize for my own behavior, Pastor," Cole said formally.

Pastor. Amanda felt chilled at his tone. Was he going through with this date for politeness? Because one shouldn't be rude to a minister? It was absurd. Would he have kept the date if he'd argued with another woman as he had with her?

"Apology accepted," Amanda said coolly, brushing stray hairs from her face. "And if that's what's bothering you, there's no need for you to feel you must keep our date."

"Don't you want to go?"

Amanda didn't know what to say. "Yes, I'd like to go, but..."

"Then we'd better leave. I made a reservation."

She stood looking at him for a moment. He waited, his brown eyes upon her, placid and unreadable. She turned and reached for her purse.

Cole walked close beside her to the truck. For the first time Amanda noticed he'd not come alone. A young man alighted from the passenger side of the truck. He opened the door for her, grinning easily. Her first thought was that Cole was so uptight, he'd brought along a chaperon.

"My little brother, Billy," Cole said, making the introductions. "Little" was stretching things a bit. Billy looked to be maybe ten years younger, but was a good head taller, than Cole. "We're giving him a lift to Union City."

"Amanda Jameson." Billy nodded politely, still grinning as he slipped beside her. "I may just begin going to church again."

Amanda answered his easy smile, his manner doing much to put her at ease. "I thank you for the compliment—I think." She laughed.

"Yes, ma'am. I see now why big brother here is so prompt to work every day." Cole cut his eyes to Billy, not commenting, and Billy went on as if he hadn't noticed. "Course, for years I've been smart enough to follow after Cole. He always spots the pretty women first. You wouldn't happen to have a sister, would you?"

"No—only three brothers."

"Are they big? Maybe Cole should be careful."

Amanda laughed. "They're all tall, but exceedingly skinny."

"Still, Cole, you'd better watch it."

Cole pulled from the road and into the gas station. "Billy, hush up and pump the gas while I pay Tate." His voice was sharp.

Billy's eyes widened, and he glanced to Cole who was already slipping from the seat. "Yes, sir." Billy gave a mock salute. Amanda glanced to her hands in her lap.

Minutes later they were back on the road and Billy was again talking. Amanda was glad. She didn't know what she would have said to Cole. She sat right beside him and it was as if a thin wall of ice separated them.

"A guy was telling me the other day a good way to meet girls was in church," Billy said. "Any truth in this, Amanda?"

"I'm sure there's a lot of truth in it, but I understand another good place is the grocery store—the meat counter," Amanda countered lightly.

"No kidding?"

She nodded seriously. "So my brother, Mark, tells me. Says he goes in and looks helpless, then asks a likely looking woman's help. Of course, this has the nasty drawback of time. How long can a person hang around the meat counter?"

"I think that would be a problem." Billy grinned. "But it could be interesting."

Amanda enjoyed the banter, but was fully aware, even if Billy wasn't, that with every comment, Cole's expression drew darker. Fifteen minutes later they dropped Billy at a friend's house. Amanda was both sorry and glad. She hoped now Cole would relax, and was fearful because she couldn't think of anything to say. Apparently neither could he.

"Have you . . ."

"Is it . . ."

They both began after a few minutes and stopped, waiting for the other.

"You first," Amanda said, laughing. At least he smiled. His smile was like the sun peeking from a cloud.

"Have you been to Christopher's?" Cole's tone was polite. He, too, was searching desperately for something to say.

I never should have come, Amanda thought. "No," she answered.

It was thirty minutes into Oklahoma City and the restaurant, and the drive was strained. They finally managed to get a conversation going—about the weather, the wheat crop, Mexican food—things people generally talk of when they have absolutely nothing to say to one another—or are afraid to talk to one another.

No matter how hard Amanda tried to relax and put Cole at ease, matters seemed to go from bad to worse. Cole's words were calculatingly polite, stiff, formal and steered away from anything personal. Amanda realized she was answering in the same fashion. Again and again she asked herself why he had invited her. Why had she accepted? They were behaving like two automatons who had no feelings—or at least denying they had any.

And Amanda did have feelings, deep, sharp feelings. She was aware of Cole's every move, the way he stroked his mustache with his forefinger, the tilt of his head, his strong hand when he reached for the gear shift knob. She felt her body's response, but couldn't understand what was happening to her.

It didn't get any better as the evening wore on.

Cole opened the door in the parking lot, but carefully avoided any physical contact. It appeared so obvious that Amanda almost gave in to a jittery laugh. The waitress asked if they wished a cocktail before dinner. Cole gruffly ordered coffee and glanced at Amanda.

"Would you like iced tea or a soft drink?"

"Oh . . . I think I'll have a glass of wine. White, please." Amanda smiled sweetly first to the waitress and then to Cole. She did it to needle him; she knew she did. But heaven knows she needed the wine. Her stomach would never accept food without some sort of digestive aid, and the wine would calm her nerves.

Cole regarded Amanda steadily for a moment, then told the waitress, "Make that two glasses, please."

Amanda glanced around the beautiful restaurant and then out the plate-glass window beside them to a small pond beyond.

"It's beautiful," she commented.

"Yes."

Silence stretched thick. Ducks swam serenely by and the leaves of the trees, tinged golden by the western sun, quivered in a light breeze. The waitress brought their drinks.

"Do you come here often?" Amanda asked.

"I've been, but I wouldn't call it often."

The low-lighted atmosphere was perfect for relaxation, but the mood seemed unable to penetrate the tension surrounding their table.

Amanda rarely drank wine and sipped it slowly, aware of her empty stomach. In a matter of minutes, it succeeded in its mellowing effect, perhaps a bit too much. Between stilted comments she found herself openly staring at Cole, studying his features.

His eyes were very brown. Deer eyes, Amanda thought. His neatly trimmed beard looked invitingly soft. She longed to see if it were so.

"Did it take you a long time to grow your beard?" she asked impulsively.

"A few months."

"Mae told me you wore a beard to cover scars from Vietnam."

"I've a few scars. Much worse than what John did today." He grinned slightly. "The scars aren't really so bad, but after I grew the beard, I discovered I liked having it."

"It does have a dashing effect," Amanda observed.

"The ladies seem to like it," he said, keeping down the smile tugging at the corners of his mouth. "Is the wine good?"

"Yes...very." Amanda peered at him over the rim of the crystal glass as she finished the last sip. "I imagine they do—the ladies, I mean. You've never been married?"

"No," he said slowly. "The only time I've ever been close, I escaped into the army."

"Escaped?"

"I was about to make a grave mistake once, and fortunately I realized it in time—about fifteen minutes before the wedding in fact. With the girl and her parents waiting at the church, I figured I'd better leave for a while. Enlisting in the army seemed the surest way."

Amanda looked at him wide-eyed, then let out a chuckle. "You both must have been very young."

"About Steven's and Marcy's age. The girl, Lori, ended up going to college, becoming a dentist, marrying a dentist and settling down in a big house with lots of little future dentists to take care of." His eyes were warm upon her as he held up his empty glass. "Perhaps you'd like another glass?"

"No...yes, perhaps I would."

His twinkling eyes upon Amanda, Cole signaled the waitress. "Another glass for the lady, please."

What was he finding so funny? Amanda wondered, smiling back at him.

Cole ordered a steak, Amanda, fish. And surprisingly she was hungry. In fact, she found the dinner delicious. As the night closed in beyond the window, the restaurant took on a romantic tone. Cole's brown eyes glowed luminously in the candlelight of their table, and he seemed to be smiling quite a bit. Their talk went easier. She could be quite witty when she put her mind to it, Amanda thought as she sipped the golden liquid and it warmed its way across her tongue and down to her stomach.

"You've never married, Amanda?" Cole asked, his eyes thoughtful, scrutinizing.

"No." Amanda reddened under his gaze. Her mind seemed intent on intimate subjects as she looked at him.

"What happened? Did your three skinny brothers chase all the boys away?"

Amanda grinned. "No, actually they ran ads in the paper and paraded on street corners trying in vain to give me away." She looked into her glass thoughtfully. "I guess I've just never taken the time. It seems odd now. So many of my friends, all of them in fact, are settled one way or the other with families, homes of their own."

"And you were always wanting to see what was over the horizon," Cole stated.

"Yes, that's a good way of putting it."

Cole nodded knowingly and smiled. In that brief instant, Amanda felt very close to him. It was a sensation she felt she could almost hold in her hand and she wished very much the moment would freeze. But as all moments do, it passed, leaving her wondering about herself and about Cole.

They were just finishing their meal when a deep male voice hailed Cole across the restaurant. A bull of a man approached, tugging a tall redheaded woman behind him. He was dressed in a blue western suit, with a string tie held by a husky gold nugget at his neck. The woman's sleek dress formed a V nearly to her navel. Her face would have made a terrific cosmetics ad, so perfect was her makeup. Amanda stared up at the woman in awe.

"Cole Mattox!" The big man affably slapped Cole on the back. "Haven't seen you in... Well, it's been a hell of a long time, buddy. Where you been keeping?"

"Hello, Val," Cole said, rising and shaking the man's hand. "I've been busy out at the ranch."

The man, Val, looked pointedly at Cole's bandage. "What kind of business, buddy? I thought you said you were settling down and through with the rowdy life." He gave a husky laugh.

Cole rubbed his bandage. "Yeah, well..."

Val turned a florid smiling face to Amanda. "And I bet this is part of what's been keeping ya. Hi do, ma'am." Val grabbed one of Amanda's hands in his big paw. "My, I sure can see Cole has found himself a gem."

Amanda felt strangely myopic, and fleeting impressions bombarded her. The redhead smiled alluringly at Cole and leaned an arm on his shoulder. Amanda looked down. The man's big paw still held her hand, and several oversize gold nugget rings with cluster diamonds sparkled before her eyes. Val rather pulled her up and bent his face to hers at the same time. Amanda's head swam. The strong reek of whiskey touched her face. In a fluid movement his hands pawed her body, stroking down her back.

Somewhat in shock, Amanda stared at Val. The next instant Cole slipped to her side. Separating her from the man, he wrapped a protective arm about her shoulders.

"Possessive, are ya now, Cole? Don't blame ya." Val hugged the redhead. "I feel the same about Tammy here." Someone called from the party at the round table and Tammy tugged at Val's hand. Val said, "Good seeing you, Cole. Look me up now, ya hear?"

Releasing Amanda, Cole pulled several bills from his pocket and tossed them to the table. "Let's go," he said shortly.

Amanda nodded and reached for her purse. She almost lost her balance, and her legs felt curiously rubbery. Cole's hand clamped her elbow, holding her close as he marched her out of the restaurant. He didn't even give her time to reply to the hostess who so considerately wished them a good evening. Amanda looked at him and blinked. What in the world was wrong? A minute before he'd been smiling. Now his jaw was as stiff as carved stone.

"Would you please slow down?" Exasperated, Amanda attempted to tug her arm from his grasp.

Cole slowed, but kept a tight hold on her arm. The knuckles of his hand brushed her breast and her skin tingled. She was exceedingly aware of the taut muscles of his thigh touching hers as they walked. He opened the passenger door, helped Amanda inside and assisted her with the seat belt. His hand brushed her abdomen. He lifted his face, and they looked at each other. Amanda tentatively touched her fingertips to the bruise beneath his eye, then brought her fingers down to his beard. She stroked it lightly, then pressed her palm against the thick hairs. It was soft.

A tremor rushed up from deep within, and her heart pounded. In a slow measured motion, Amanda brought her lips to Cole's. Conflicting thoughts tumbled over one another. Would he jerk away? What magic possessed her? Was it true magic or just a mirage? And, oh, she wanted to feel his lips against her own.

For a brief moment, his lips burned hers. She parted her mouth hungrily, and for an instant, Cole responded. Then he jerked away.

"You're drunk," he said flatly.

Amanda was aghast. "I am not drunk! I've never been drunk in my life!" Her heart pounded, and the pressure of his lips upon hers lingered. Her body ached.

"Well you are now." He slammed the door and went around to get behind the wheel.

"How dare you accuse me of such a thing!" Amanda exclaimed when he got in the truck. "For heaven's sake, I only had two small glasses of wine."

"Three."

"Okay. So you felt the need to keep score."

"How many do you normally have?" Cole asked, calmly starting the engine.

"Well…I do occasionally drink wine," Amanda hedged. She straightened her dress and laid her purse primly upon her lap. "Jesus drank wine, you know. He even went around changing water into wine."

"I thought so," Cole said knowingly. "Let's drop it, shall we?"

"Fine," Amanda agreed haughtily. Maybe he didn't care for her kisses. The thought sat there a minute. "Don't you like the way I kiss?"

Cole was pulling out into the stream of traffic on the interstate. "What?" He glanced at her briefly, his eyebrows together, and then turned his attention back to the road. "I like them fine," he answered slowly.

"Then what's wrong? Why are you so angry?"

"It's nothing. Nothing you did."

Minutes later, as they sped smoothly down the highway, Cole said, "I'm sorry about Val."

"It's okay. And thank you for stepping in."

That was all they said for thirty-five miles.

Chapter Six

Cole pulled into the driveway of the parsonage, got out and came around to open the door for Amanda. She beat him to it and slipped from the high seat to the ground. Her legs didn't feel as elastic now and her head had quit swirling. Still, Cole put a supporting hand to her arm and walked very close.

A car came down the road and slowed noticeably as it passed. Glancing quickly, Amanda thought she recognized it as belonging to Glenda Boyer. She groaned inwardly. That was all she needed.

Cole waited while she opened the front door and turned on the lamp inside.

"You don't lock this door, either?" he asked disapprovingly as he stepped into the room and glanced around.

"No. I operate on the open home theory. If people want in, they can come in and take what they want, then leave."

"That's fine as long as what they want isn't you."

"As far as I know, a crime wave has not descended on Coogan, Oklahoma."

"It only takes one time." He stepped to the door and tested the lock, setting it to fasten. "Good night," he said, turning to leave. Amanda stopped him.

"Cole." He looked at her and waited, his face an impassive mask. "Thank you for trying to show me a good time tonight. I'm sorry it didn't work out so well. I did enjoy myself for a while." She looked at him, questioning, wondering if he also had.

"I did too. Good night."

Amanda shut the door and leaned against it, listening as Cole backed out and sped off down the dirt road. Slipping off her shoes, she had a strong urge to throw them full force across the room. She resisted. Years of training. Anger solved very few things.

Calmly she changed into a cool, whisper-thin nightgown and turned up the air-conditioning. She was so hot and was sure that her anger and physical longing had something to do with it. She washed her face and brushed her teeth. She even flossed—each tooth. Methodically she spread down the covers and fluffed her pillows.

Suddenly her fingers closed around one pillow and it went hurtling across the room. It slammed into the closet door with a thundering rattle. Amanda felt such satisfaction that she did it with her other pillow as well. She was so mad! Mad at Cole, mad at herself, mad at the world in general. Confusion overwhelmed her.

Tonight she had acted like a stupid child, trying to prove some point. What point? If Cole couldn't see she was a woman, then the man was blind!

And she'd kissed him. Again she wondered about the precise definition of a kiss. Oh well, it didn't matter.

Had she actually asked him if he liked kissing her?

The fact was, she'd made a fool of herself.

It could have been worse, she reflected. She'd only had three glasses of wine and had conducted herself with at least a minimum of decorum. She'd not fallen down, totally lost her temper or torn his clothes off.

She got into bed and pulled up the covers. It wasn't even ten o'clock. She lay staring at the flowers on the sheet, seeing only scenes from the evening.

And wanting Cole.

The telephone rang. Absently Amanda reached for it. "Hello."

"Hello." Immediately Amanda tensed, recognizing the low gravelly voice. "Look," he said, "I think I need to explain something, clear the air. It has nothing to do with you being a minister. Well, not much. I admit it did come as a surprise, but that's not the problem. I'm just not ready for any kind of commitment, any kind of serious involvement at all. I like my life free and loose—no strings."

Amanda pondered that for a moment. The line hummed faintly with Cole's breathing. "So? I don't remember either of us saying anything about ropes, strings or marriage—engagement even."

"You don't have to say it." Irritation edged his voice. "Permanence—home and slippers—sticks out all over you like a neon sign."

Amanda pulled back the receiver and looked at it. The gall of the man! He certainly had an enormous ego if he thought she was so smitten with him she was ready for the altar.

"If you'd take a good look at that neon sign, you'd notice it was off. I, too, am not looking for any sort of serious involvement. Besides, I think it wise to get to know someone before contemplating marriage."

"Good. Considering our reactions to each other in the past, I think the wise, adult thing to do is to stay out of each other's way."

"I couldn't agree more. Good night."

"Good night."

Amanda turned out the light, then snuggled down in the sheets and punched her pillow, trying to get comfortable. What did permanence look like anyway? "Nothing to do with me being a minister, my eye," she mumbled disgustedly.

Cole lay in bed, staring at the pattern the moonlight made on the sheets. He knew perfectly well what bothered him was the fact Amanda was a minister. He had to admit the truth to himself, even if he couldn't admit it to her. He felt childish.

His chest tightened as he thought angrily of Lyle Winfield. Damn him! Cole would get him back if it was the last thing he did. He'd like to punch his face in, but he wasn't about to give Lyle any satisfaction. He'd simply remain quiet and act as if nothing had happened. Then at least Lyle would be denied the good laugh he was hoping for.

Besides, if word got out that he was trying to make time with her, Amanda could be hurt. Cole didn't want that. The hurt he'd seen on her face when he'd picked her up had been enough. He found he wanted to protect her and make her smile. Fleetingly he recalled the softness of her skin and the feminine curves of her body pressed to his.

But he didn't want to get involved. No, not with her.

Yet he didn't much like the idea of her being with someone else. The easy way Amanda and Billy had got on nettled him. What was wrong with Billy? Couldn't he see that she was... Well, that he shouldn't talk to a minister that way?

Cole let out a dispirited sigh. The fact was, for the past year or so he'd been looking for a woman to settle down and raise a family with. He'd thought of his dream woman when he'd planned his house, hoping to please her with the layout of the kitchen and a fireplace in the bedroom.

And in the past days he'd sort of begun to see Amanda as that woman.

But not now. Oh, no, not now. He simply couldn't see himself in any kind of relationship with the Reverend Amanda Jameson.

Amanda stayed away from the church as much as possible the following week. When she did happen to be there at the same time as Cole, it was only for a few short minutes. She didn't venture to the south wing, and Cole stayed away from the north. All through the week she tried to sort out her feelings. Why was she angry? And whom was she angry at: Cole or herself?

On Monday she spoke to Lowry about having her name fully spelled out on a new sign. That very afternoon she saw Cole working on it. There, she thought with satisfaction, no more mistakes.

Wednesday, she found a batch of invoices for building materials on her desk. She totaled them, wrote a check, then sat tapping the check against her palm, wondering what she should do with it. Mailing the check was out of the question. It just seemed too silly. But she didn't want to face Cole.

She contemplated this cowardly emotion for several minutes. Then, rising purposefully, she strode from her office. Amanda Jameson was not one to avoid facing anything, be it a person, an unpleasant encounter or her own stupidity.

Her determination was admirable, but unnecessary. Cole was nowhere about, though his truck sat parked in its usual place. With a sigh and a shrug, Amanda placed the check on the dashboard.

Friday, dressed in jeans and an old cotton shirt, Amanda was painting the back deck of the parsonage when Mae Loggin appeared.

"You're a pretty picture," Mae teased. "I should take a snapshot and show it at the next meeting of the Ladies Club. I could entitle it, Our Preacher at Work."

Amanda grinned and wiped her paint-stained hands. "Glad to see you, Mae. I need a break."

"Enjoyed your sermon Sunday on controlling one's temper," Mae said, as Amanda joined her at the kitchen table with glasses of tea. "Too bad John Tidwell didn't come to hear it. Don't be upset about him, Amanda. He'll come around eventually. Underneath all that spleen, John's a reasonable man."

Amanda smiled wanly. "John came to see me Sunday afternoon. We talked. We didn't agree, but we talked and made a truce."

Mae eyed her closely, and Amanda stirred sugar into her tea, avoiding the older woman's eyes.

"Okay, so what's up? And don't try to brush me off. You've got frown wrinkles between your eyebrows. You might as well know, Glenda Boyer has made it known that she saw you and Cole, very cozy, in front of the parsonage last Friday night. She even went so far as to return and make sure Cole's truck had gone."

Amanda's eyes widened and she blinked. She'd not heard so much as a whisper of gossip. "You're awfully blunt, you know that, Mae?"

"I gave up subtlety on my fiftieth birthday."

Amanda sipped her tea. She could make up something, but she really needed to talk. Maybe it would clear up the jumble of emotions that kept whirling around in her brain. Besides, when Mae had something on her mind, she was as persistent as a dog worrying a bone.

"I didn't preach that sermon just for John Tidwell. I guess I was speaking more to myself. I lost my temper with Cole Mattox and said some things.... Oh, Mae, of all people, I should know better. I should have better control."

"Goodness. What happened?"

"Mae, he didn't know I was the minister. I know it sounds crazy, but he really didn't know and when he found out ... well, we sort of had a fight."

Mae looked incredulous. Then a low chuckle began. "He didn't know?" She chuckled even harder.

"It's not all that funny, Mae. He thought I was the secretary, that perhaps A. J. Jameson was my father or uncle or something. And there was no one to tell him any different, because no one knew he didn't know," Amanda said miserably. The whole thing sounded even more confusing and unbelievable when put into words. "He found out when I asked him to witness Steven and Marcy's wedding."

Mae still chuckled. "And then he got socked in the eye on top of it." The older woman looked curious. "It came as quite a shock, I imagine."

"To say the least—for both of us. He acted like I'd done something deceitful. He said all sorts of stupid things about the way I looked, the way I acted. With his attitude coming right after that scene with John— Well, I got on my high horse and lost my temper. I'm so ashamed of my behavior."

"So what were you two doing together—cozy—Friday night?"

Amanda sighed, then related the story of their date and the fiasco it had been. The only thing she didn't mention was kissing him, though she remembered it explicitly. "I think deep down I wanted to show him that I was a human being. I wanted him to see me as a woman, not a category. I ended up showing him a silly child."

Mae touched Amanda's hand. "Childish perhaps, but human." A woman crazy over a man, Mae thought to herself.

"It's a common enough reaction, Mae, but this is the first time it's hurt so badly. I'm still me. I'm still the person he talked to so readily about automobiles and the church's construction. I'm still the person who fought the fire with everyone else. Why does me being a minister make such a difference?"

"Because it brought Cole up against the fact that you would take any relationship seriously, that you wouldn't be playing around. Honey, Cole's been running away from things for the past ten years: from life, from responsibility, from himself. Coming home, building a house and farm, he's trying now to make a stand, but he feels shaky, especially when commitment to another person is involved. And, obviously, he's stereotyping you. And if he does that, he must stereotype himself. He can't see fitting in."

Amanda quietly reviewed Mae's words. Then she looked at the older woman earnestly. "Something happens when we're together, Mae. It's like going to the circus or driving the Jeep full out over slick sand. I feel an added degree of life." She looked down at her glass. "It's kind of scary. And I don't know what to do about it."

"Would you say you're in love with him, Amanda?"

"I don't know what love is," Amanda said quietly. "I felt what I thought was love once, but I never had a chance to find out."

"And you regret it?"

"I did for a while. But there wasn't anything I could do about it." Sighing, Amanda rose to look out the kitchen window. The bright yellow black-eyed Susans along the fence waved gently in the breeze.

"I've let love pass me by. I did it by choice. I've known since I was a child and chose to be a minister that I couldn't have both my ministry and a family." Turning to face Mae, Amanda leaned against the counter. "Oh, I know there are some women who manage to do it all, and quite successfully. But it just wouldn't work for me. The ministry is a life commitment. I thought I'd made the right decision until I met Paul—a man I met in Mexico. Then I began to doubt, to realize what I had given up."

They both sat silently. Then Mae said, "Give Cole a chance, Amanda."

Amanda smiled tightly. "I don't think Cole is the only one afraid of involvement and more than a mite confused. And I think the best thing for both of us, given the volatile happenings every time we come together, is to stay away from each other. Cole has made his feelings very clear; he wants nothing to do with this preacher lady."

For days Mae deliberated on a way to bring Amanda and Cole together. All the two needed was a nudge, just a tiny one. And she wasn't meddling. She was simply helping nature along.

She considered and discarded at least a hundred inspirations. Every idea had a serious flaw. There had to be a foolproof way of getting them together at the same time, where it would be too awkward for either to beg off.

As it happened, the perfect incident came about entirely on its own. But Mae preferred to believe she "thought" it into happening. With just a bit of help, every detail fell magically into place, as if she'd ordered it from above, and Mae felt extremely smug about the whole matter.

On Thursday afternoon, Mae pulled up in front of the Coogan Diner, where she'd arranged to meet Amanda for lunch. Gray clouds overcast the sky, and a high wind blew. Mae opened her car door, intending to make a sprint for the diner.

It was unclear in her mind exactly how she did it, but stepping out of the car, Mae caught her right heel on the floorboard. Losing her balance, she grabbed frantically for the door handle, clutched it momentarily, then it broke off in her hand as she tumbled to the ground. Her foot wrenched and remained stuck in the car. Plastic handles! she seethed inwardly, an involuntary cry of pain escaping her lips.

"Mae?" She heard Amanda call, and then came the crunch of steps running across the gravel.

But it wasn't only Amanda. Cole appeared, coming from the grocery store, Mae imagined by the way he approached.

Mae looked up into their concerned faces. Amanda took the broken, plastic door handle from her grip. Mae made sure her face registered intense agony. Gently Cole lifted her ankle from the car and helped her move to a more prone position. Amanda took Mae's head upon her knees.

"Mae," Cole asked in his steady, gruff voice as his hands methodically checked her leg, "how bad is it?" Gently he tested her ankle.

"I think it's—" she gasped, for it did hurt "—broken."

Amanda pressed her palm against Mae's forehead, then checked the older woman's pulse. Mae allowed her hand to dangle weakly. By now, several more people had gathered.

"Does it hurt anywhere besides your ankle, Mae?" Amanda asked.

Take 4 Books
–and a Mystery Gift–
FREE

**And preview exciting new Silhouette Romance novels
every month — as soon as they're published!**

Silhouette Romance®

Yes...Get 4 Silhouette Romance novels (a $7.80 value) along with your Mystery Gift FREE

SLIP AWAY FOR AWHILE... Let Silhouette Romance draw you into a love-filled world of fascinating men and women. You'll find it's easy to close the door on the cares and concerns of everyday life as you lose yourself in the timeless drama of love, played out in exotic locations the world over.

EVERY BOOK AN ORIGINAL... Every Silhouette Romance is a full-length story, never before in print, superbly written to give you more of what you want from romance. Start with 4 brand new Silhouette Romance novels—yours free with the attached coupon. Along with your Mystery Gift, it's a $7.80 gift from us to you, with no obligation to buy anything now or ever.

YOUR FAVORITE AUTHORS... Silhouette Romance novels are created by the very best authors of romantic fiction. Let your favorite authors—such as Brittany Young, Diana Palmer, Janet Dailey, Nora Roberts, and many more—take you to a whole other world.

ROMANCE-FILLED READING... Each month you'll meet lively young heroines and share in their trials and triumphs...bold, virile men you'll find as fascinating as the heroines do...and colorful supporting characters you'll feel you've known forever. They're all in Silhouette Romance novels—and now you can share every one of the wonderful reading adventures they provide.

NO OBLIGATION... Each month we'll send you 6 brand-new Silhouette Romance novels. Your books will be sent to you as soon as they are published, without obligation. If not enchanted, simply return them within 15 days and owe nothing. Or keep them, and pay just $1.95 each (a total of $11.70). And there's never an additional charge for shipping and handling.

SPECIAL EXTRAS FOR HOME SUBSCRIBERS ONLY... When you take advantage of this offer and become a home subscriber, we'll also send you the Silhouette Books Newsletter FREE with each book shipment. Every informative issue features news about upcoming titles, interviews with your favorite authors, even their favorite recipes.

So send in the postage-paid card today, and take your fantasies further than they've ever been. The trip will do you good!

CLIP AND MAIL COUPON TODAY!

NO POSTAGE
NECESSARY
IF MAILED
IN THE
UNITED STATES

BUSINESS REPLY CARD

FIRST CLASS   PERMIT NO. 194   CLIFTON, N.J.

Postage will be paid by addressee

Silhouette Books
120 Brighton Road
P.O. BOX 5084
Clifton, NJ 07015-9956

"My leg..." Mae managed. This incident had been thrown in her lap. It was up to her to do her best. Glancing up, she caught the look of consultation that passed between Cole and Amanda. Cole nodded slightly. Mae closed her eyes in satisfaction. Amanda looks so pretty in that burgundy sweater, she thought. It makes her eyes shine.

"I think it's the hospital for you, Mae," Amanda said. "Where's Lowry?"

"He went to Tulsa this morning. Won't be home until tomorrow." Her hand waving vaguely in the air was a nice touch, she thought.

Her ankle throbbed and Mae truly grimaced as Amanda helped Cole lift her into his arms.

"The Jeep," Amanda said, and quickly went to open the door and move the front seat aside. The rear seat was short, but so was Mae. Amanda folded a wool blanket for Mae to prop her ankle and took Mae's head on her lap. Cole drove, leaving the parking lot in a flurry of spraying gravel.

"He'll have us there before you know it," Amanda said, stroking the hair from Mae's forehead.

Mae looked up with a smile she hoped was sufficiently weak. Actually her ankle felt better, though a bit numb.

Twenty-five minutes later, Cole helped lift Mae onto a stretcher, and she was rolled into the emergency room. The two young people were left standing side by side, their faces pinched in concern. Mae had to suppress a smile. It was all working out wonderfully.

The doctor on call examined her, but she insisted her own physician, Harold Rosenblitt, be called. Forty minutes later, he arrived and studied her X rays. Mae, feeling more comfortable after pain medication, reclined on the emergency bed, drinking coffee.

"It's not broken, but it is sprained," Dr. Rosenblitt said as he jotted notes on Mae's chart. "We'll get it bandaged up in a minute. Go home and keep it propped up for a few days. We'll get you some crutches, too."

"I want you to keep me here overnight," Mae said.

Harold Rosenblitt's eyebrows shot up and he put the chart aside. "You want what?"

"I want you to keep me here overnight," Mae repeated calmly. "You know . . . at my age . . ."

Rosenblitt snorted and crossed his arms. "You're healthier than a woman half your age. Are you going to tell me the reason for this request?"

"Of course, Harold," Mae said sweetly. "Later. Right now just remember who raised half the money for the obstetrics wing."

Harold Rosenblitt grunted and turned away. "Blackmail!"

Amanda watched with a sense of helplessness as Mae was wheeled through the swinging doors and out of sight. She sat in a chair before the emergency desk and answered questions while the secretary typed the answers on a form. Cole stood silently behind her, a strong supportive presence.

When the questions finished, Amanda and Cole wandered about the waiting room, neither content to sit for long. Though they said little, Amanda was grateful Cole was there with her.

Minutes later there came a flurry of activity. Several nurses and orderlies ran out from behind the swinging doors, down the hall, and then, seconds later, returned. More people came, pushing a cart bearing electronic equipment. Her heart jumping to her throat, Amanda asked the desk clerk what was going on. The clerk went to find out. In a minute she returned and assured Amanda that Mae Loggin was fine. The crash cart had been for another patient.

Amanda and Cole waited.

Mae was Amanda's surrogate mother, the sister she had never had and a dear friend. At this moment, Amanda felt terribly shaky. She feared losing Mae. After all, Mae was seventy years old. It was at least a wrenched ankle, could be much more. Amanda rose to lean against the wall and offered up a rather confused prayer. A tear escaped and trickled down her cheek. Seeing Cole look over at her, Amanda turned her face and hastily wiped away the tear. But he'd already seen.

He walked over to her and stood uneasily, his hands jammed in his pockets. "She'll be okay," he said. The next second Cole's strong arms were around her, pulling her to him. "She'll be okay," he repeated in his gruff voice. "There's no reason to think she won't be unless we receive word otherwise."

Amanda burrowed her face into the stiff warmth of his denim jacket. He smelled faintly of manly cologne, wood chips and human body scent all mixed. She willed the tears not to start and swallowed past the lump in her throat. Cole stroked her hair then lifted her face, his hands cradling her cheeks.

"We know she hurt her ankle." His brown eyes regarded her firmly. "Nothing more. Don't go jumping the gun with negative thoughts. It won't do any good."

Amanda nodded, managing a smile. "You're absolutely right," she said, attempting to match his firmness. "Thanks for the reminder."

"Good." With his arm around her shoulder, Cole guided her to a chair. "Now sit there. I'll get us a couple of Cokes."

Fifteen minutes later, a young nurse came out. "Mrs. Loggin is resting comfortably. She's asked for her own physician and this will take a while. You two should have time to go for coffee or a bite to eat,'' the nurse suggested, glancing to her watch. "Say an hour.''

"You haven't had any lunch, have you?'' Cole asked.

Amanda shook her head. "I was meeting Mae for lunch.''

Cole took her elbow. "I haven't, either. Come on.'' He held her arm all the way to the hospital restaurant.

Because of the report that Mae was resting comfortably and the nurse's manner, Amanda relaxed. She and Cole talked easily, over a lunch of club sandwiches and coffee. It seemed odd, since they had parted on such a strained note two weeks ago. Remembering, Amanda smiled inwardly and lowered her eyes. She'd only caught a distant glimpse of Cole in all that time. It was nice being with him again.

She allowed her gaze to flow over his face, taking in the rich softness of his beard, the fading yellow and blue bruise below his left eye; noting several gray strands of hair at his temple.

They discussed how Mae must have fallen, and Cole told several entertaining stories about Mae from when he was a child. One time he had so infuriated her by accidentally mowing down a corner of a bed of mums that she'd actually chased him up a tree. She came right up after me,'' Cole said. "And she was closing in on fifty years old at the time. The only thing that saved me was that Mae got up on the branch and suddenly realized where she was. I had to promise to help her down and never tell a soul.''

Amanda laughed until tears shone in her eyes. "And now you've broken that promise,'' she teased. "Wait until I tell.'' Yes, it was good to be with Cole, Amanda thought, as the waitress refilled their coffee cups. She smiled at him and he smiled easily in return.

A few minutes after they'd returned to the emergency waiting room, a tall, robust man with thick, salt-and- pepper hair appeared and walked over to them. "Amanda

Jameson? Cole Mattox?" Amanda nodded and the man held out his hand. "Dr. Harold Rosenblitt. Mae's fine, except for a severely sprained ankle." He coughed into his fist. "These sprains can sometimes turn out to be worse than a clean break. But she's fine . . . fine. I just want to keep her overnight as a precaution."

"Oh." The word came out small. Amanda wasn't completely reassured. The doctor seemed to be hiding something.

Mae came through the swinging doors, riding regally in a wheelchair, her ankle bandaged and propped out straight. She looked pale, but not quite so weak. If anything, she seemed rather content at the moment. Amanda wanted to stay and see Mae to her room, but the older woman insisted she return with Cole.

"Then I'll be back later. I can bring your night things, books, anything you'd like me to get for you," Amanda said.

"I'm only here for the night, Amanda. The hospital will provide everything I need." Mae waved her purse. "I have money for a new toothbrush and anything else I may take into my head to want. Don't worry about Lowry. I'll call him straight away and tell him what I've gotten into. Now shoo. You two get. Looks like it'll pour any minute."

Dr. Rosenblitt took the handles of Mae's chair. "Mae needs rest," he said. "You can come for her tomorrow morning around ten."

It was just after three o'clock, but already growing dim as heavy purple clouds blanketed the sky. Amanda was thankful she'd put the canvas top on the Jeep that morning. She slipped behind the wheel as Cole slid into the passenger seat. Now that she was not so worried about Mae, Amanda was surprised at her reaction to Cole sitting so close. She was so aware of him she felt she could hear his heart beating, and he hers. The air felt sticky, and perspiration tingled the back of her neck and between her breasts.

Minutes later it began to rain, lightly at first, then heavier, falling in sheets across the windshield and drumming hard upon the canvas. A strong north wind buffeted the Jeep, and the wipers thumped rapidly. Amanda gripped the steering wheel.

"I think I'm going to have to pull over and wait for it to let up," she said. A giant semi passed, rocking the Jeep. Amanda fought the wheel and struggled to see through the rain.

"Might be best," Cole agreed. "There's room along here."

Suddenly two blurry red lights glowed through the wet windshield. Amanda blinked, trying to peer through the driving rain and between the swipes of the wiper blades. Again the red dots shivered before her eyes. *Brake lights.* They seemed to appear out of nowhere. Only seconds before, the gray road stretching ahead had been clear.

The glowing red spots grew even as Amanda watched, glaring with monstrous brilliance through the moisture. The vehicle ahead of her was stopped on the road. Sucking in her breath, she pressed the brakes, pumping lightly, afraid of a skid. Everything was happening so quickly there wasn't time to think, only to react. And somewhere in there a plea for help was offered up.

Her hands gripped the wheel tightly, but not rigidly. Again she pressed with the flat of her boot, testing the brake. It wasn't enough. She pressed harder, downshifted and searched the shoulder, straining...straining to see.

Then the Jeep began to skid. The back end waved back and forth, as if trying to make up its mind which way to go. Then it chose one way while the front went the other—toward the oncoming lane. With both hands, Amanda tugged hard on the wheel, turning to the right. Lights shone blindingly, horns honked and the Jeep swerved back into the proper lane, then off the pavement onto the grassy shoulder. It bumped across the rough ground as if it were now driving itself.

Chapter Seven

The Jeep took the sloping bank of the ditch easily, following it as if it were the road. Off the slick pavement at last, Amanda fairly stood on the brake. The tires skidded, this time in slick, wet grass. For one breathless instant, the Jeep tilted, the two left wheels spinning in the air, then it bounced down again on all fours and stopped—finally.

They were safe, still in one piece. Cars passed up on the highway, their lights distorted through the film of water.

Amanda took a tentative breath, then a good full one. The engine purred smoothly. The glass was fogging, and rain beat on the canvas roof and fell as a raging river across the windshield. Amanda's pulse pounded in her ears and her hands shook ever so slightly. Cutting the ignition, she leaned her head against the seat, moving her mouth to offer thanks, but the words sounded only in her heart. She couldn't speak yet. Stretching her fingers, she released her hold on the steering wheel. Her hands ached from strain.

"Yep," Cole's voice broke the stillness. "There's room along here to pull off."

Slowly Amanda turned to him. He sat calmly with one arm draped across his knee. A grin tugged at the corners of his mouth. She shook her head, pressing her lips against an incredulous smile.

"I believe we could safely term this one of your miracles, Amanda. Helped along by your skill, of course."

"Skill? Thanks for the compliment, but that was pure miracle. No doubt about it." Her hands shook and she was terribly cold. She blew onto her hands and rubbed them together, and kept telling herself they were okay, still in one piece, no blood, no pain.

Cole took her hands in his and rubbed them briskly. "Cold?" His brown eyes filled with concern.

Amanda nodded.

Cole didn't take his hands from hers. Amanda looked down at them. They were large enough to fully encompass her own, even to hide them. He shifted in his seat, removing one of his hands from hers, making room for her. Then he drew her into the shelter of his arms. Amanda went willingly.

She leaned against his shoulder and Cole rested the side of his chin on her head. His breath teased her hair. It was terribly quiet with only the sound of heavy pattering raindrops against the Jeep. Sheets of water enveloped them, isolated them in a world all their own. With the heavy downpour, it grew darker, and the windows fogged from the moisture and their breath.

Even through his denim jacket and cotton shirt, Amanda felt the rock hardness of Cole's chest, the steady beat of his heart. Virtually pinned by the strength of his taut arms, there was no way she could move. And she didn't want to.

His embrace sheltered her and she felt wanted. She was warm; her whole body throbbed with warmth.

Time stood still. They neither moved nor spoke—not audibly. But between their touching bodies passed a message more vivid, more explicit than words. Amanda felt as if she'd known Cole all her life. She remembered the feel of his lips on hers and the fire that had coursed so magically through every part of her body. Never in all her life had Amanda been more aware of a man. She knew, and instinct told her he did too, that she dare not move, dare not turn her face to his. Between them burned a closely banked fire hovering threateningly on the edge of eruption.

Amanda gave her mind up to simply and completely cherishing the moment.

Then gradually Cole moved, bringing his head down to hers. Amanda turned to meet him, parting her lips in anticipation. Fleetingly, before his lids closed to hide them, Cole's eyes revealed a sense of wonder, of longing. Or was it simply a reflection of her own feelings?

His lips massaged hers, burning and demanding, then pressing her mouth open, he entered her with his tongue. And Amanda answered with equal force. His hand stroked her thigh, burning through the fabric. Wanting to experience all of him, she pressed against him, a throbbing wetness welling up between her legs and spreading throughout her body. His strong, firm touch moved to her inner thigh, sending her mind into a whirling orbit.

Cole, her mind called longingly. Cole, it whispered.

She was sure her breath was gone and did not care. Then Cole broke away. His eyes were hot pinpoints as his gaze moved the length of her body. He looked away.

Amanda laid her head on his chest, feeling his trembling muscles, the ragged rise and fall of his chest and the rapid beating of his heart.

What was he thinking? Did he feel as she did? Obviously his body did, but did Cole, with his whole being, long for her as she did for him?

How long they sat there, Amanda had no idea. Gradually she became aware of the pounding rain becoming only a drizzle and of the storm's mock darkness lifting. Cole moved a hand to stroke her hair.

"We'd better get going," he said, his voice husky.

Amanda wanted to look at him, to read what was written in his eyes. But she couldn't bring her gaze to meet his. It was silly, yet she couldn't. What if she didn't like what she saw? She just couldn't risk letting him see her face at that moment; her vulnerablity was there for all to see.

"Yes," she said simply, her voice barely above a whisper.

She let Cole out at Coogan Grocery. "Thanks," he offered, pulling up the collar of his denim jacket. "Drive carefully." Then he was out and sprinting through the drizzle to his truck. His words were polite nothings. They'd driven most of the way to Coogan in silence. It had been an odd silence, strained, yet not distant.

Amanda pulled onto the road, leaving Cole sitting behind the wheel of his truck, the engine not yet started. The Jeep plowed its way off the county blacktop and down the dirt road, which ran with water, and up the driveway to the parsonage. She dashed through the rain and in the back door, which was unlocked as usual. The house greeted her, cool, damp and empty. Rubbing her arms, Amanda pulled logs and kindling from the box beside the hearth and began laying a fire. She was so cold, and the house seemed so empty. Rain pattered against the roof, and the mantel clock ticked loudly in the silence. Then the rumble of an engine filtered through the windows.

Rising slowly, Amanda looked out the front window. Cole's truck sat in the driveway, Cole himself silhouetted in the seat. Amanda waited, wanting very much for him to come in, to talk with him, to be with him. Give us a chance to know one another, Cole, her heart whispered. Then she looked around the room, seeing the sofa, with its nest of pillows, the promised fire in the cold fireplace, the misty rain blurring the windows. They would be alone.

She placed her palms to her burning cheeks. Cole's truck backed slowly out of the driveway. Amanda watched it go and listened as the sound of the engine faded.

She lit the kindling in the fireplace, and in a minute the carefully laid logs caught and flamed. Curling herself on the end of the couch, Amanda hugged a throw pillow to her stomach and stared into the fire. She saw before her, as clearly as though he were in the room, Cole's rough male face. She saw his thick dark beard and his equally thick and dark, neatly trimmed hair, with wisps that insisted on falling across his forehead. She recalled his muscular build, the tilt of his head and the way he tended to walk on the balls of his feet, giving his steps a jaunty air.

His eyes stared at her from the flames, dark cocoa-brown eyes, sometimes impishly, laughing, other times brooding, and so many times reflecting a warm inner kindness. She could almost feel the texture of his hair, the roughness of his work-worn hands and could almost smell the musky male scent that clung to him.

He was stubborn and a bit on the cocky side; anyone could see it. He tended to take over, just assuming that people would follow his lead and not bothering to ask anyone's leave. And he wasn't inclined to easily change his mind once he'd made a decision or to readily admit he'd been wrong, Amanda thought with a gentle smile. But she knew there was a well of strength in Cole Mattox, born of an abiding kindness.

How in the world could she know these things about him? She'd not had more than a handful of real conversations with the man.

She didn't know how she knew, only that she did. She'd seen the truth of him in his eyes, felt it in the gentle touch of his hands and could sense in a way that needed no words, the strength, the tender understanding nature of the man. This one trait, above all the others, drew her to him.

And drawn she was, no doubt about it. She longed to be with him, to be the receiver of his smiles and his touches. She was astonished at the way her senses tingled at the very thought of him—astonished, and a bit embarrassed. Throwing aside the embarrassment, Amanda looked at her feelings in wonder.

Could this be what it feels like to love a man? she thought. And what if she did?

In that crystal clear moment, Amanda felt her life taking a turn. It made her terribly uneasy. She shied away from the change, as one would from quicksand. One false step and she feared she'd be caught in something from which there was no escape. If she fell for Cole Mattox, then what of her ministry? What of the life she had given everything for all these years? And what if nothing ever came of her love? A knife twisted in Amanda's heart.

Cole jerked opened the refrigerator, pulled out ham and cheese and fairly slapped together a sandwich. He was angry at Amanda, at the incessant rain drumming on the roof of his small trailer, at his wet stinky dog, Mac, who hurried to hide under the bed, and at himself.

How could that little mite of a woman have gotten under his skin? He'd actually found himself sitting in her driveway, wanting to go to her, to feel her creamy skin and to see her smile. He wasn't completely sure he should be having thoughts such as these about a minister, even if she were a woman. His uncertainty made him feel off balance. Cole allowed himself a low, bitter chuckle. He'd start seeing her, and before he knew it, he'd be up in that little white church of hers, tied up like a neat little package.

He just couldn't see himself as the husband of a minister, though he couldn't pinpoint why. Amanda was certainly feminine—no doubt about that. But she just seemed so self-sufficient, so strong and high-handed.

The reasons sounded weak and nonsensical even to his own ears. It didn't matter, he told himself. He didn't fit at all with Amanda Jameson and that was all there was to it.

Amanda rose blurry eyed and achy, her nose stuffy. She'd not slept well, and had had to answer at least a dozen telephone calls the previous evening, all from people calling to inquire about Mae. Mae herself had even called before Amanda had had a chance to call the hospital. Lowry would be picking her up this morning. For an elderly woman with a severly sprained ankle, she'd certainly sounded chipper. And for some odd, uncomfortable reason, she'd asked if Cole were there.

The rain had let up, but the land remained shrouded by clouds. Sniffing loudly, Amanda ran water in the kettle and looked out the window. A car, an old, decrepit, possibly blue, Chevy Malibu bumped slowly down the dirt drive that bordered her fence and went to the abandoned farmhouse farther up the hill.

Amanda watched it curiously. All she could see of the driver was a dark shadowy figure who she believed was male. She'd never seen anyone up at the shack, had never even given a thought to who owned the land.

Beginning to prepare a small breakfast, Amanda sighed. It seemed so lonely, just herself. For a moment, she pictured Cole sitting across the table. Then the moment was gone. I must be more tired than I realized, she thought with a shake of her head. Her mind whirling, she'd found the loaf of bread nearly gone, though she'd been sure she had a new loaf, and the half gallon of milk she'd thought was in the refrigerator wasn't even there at all.

After a substantial breakfast and three hot cups of coffee, however, Amanda felt much revived. Her sniffles stopped, her brain cleared and even the sun tried to peek through the misty cloud. She scurried around the house, straightening up, eager to get to the church.

Cole will be there, she thought. Amanda tried to play down this incentive, but her heart sang, as if of its own accord. They were on speaking terms again. Yesterday he'd held her in his arms.

Pausing before the mirror, Amanda looked at herself. A tiny thought formed. If she could just get Cole to see her as a woman... Tossing the idea aside, she opened the closet and rummaged for something to wear. But the idea poked up again and nagged at her. Again, for a full minute, Amanda looked at her reflection. Then she tried on nearly every outfit in her closet before deciding on one that felt just right. After all, it was worth a try.

The exterior of the church's new south wing was all but completed. A bit of trim around the windows and the painting were the only things still to do. Two of Cole's brothers had helped with building the roof, and they'd finished the shingling several days before.

Another truck was parked alongside Cole's. It bore the logo, Johnson's Electric. As she walked through the sanctuary, Amanda heard the whirring of drills. The entrance to the south wing was no longer shrouded over. She walked down the hall, taking in the newly laid oak flooring and the plasterboard on the walls and ceilings of the various rooms. Following the sound of tools and voices to the last room at the end of the hall, Amanda heard the tinkle of feminine laughter at the same moment she poked her head through the doorway.

The eager zing in her heart shriveled as she saw Cole smiling easily at a tall, golden-haired woman. The woman was dressed in a slim-fitting knit shirt and overalls, and her leather-gloved hand held a screwdriver, but in no way did she look like a man. She smiled alluringly at Cole. The two were obviously enjoying one another.

Amanda would have backed away unnoticed, except for another man in the room who noticed her. "Hello," he called out with a friendly grin. Cole and the woman turned. The woman smiled openly, but a curtain seemed to fall across Cole's face, making it unreadable. He motioned her in.

"This is Pastor Jameson," he said. "Pastor, this is Neil Johnson and his sister, Courtney, the electrical contractors."

It was a jolt to hear him call her Pastor. And why did she still feel... well, unsettled as she looked at him?

She managed a smile she hoped was warm and friendly and shook hands with the two Johnsons. Neil appeared older, Courtney about Amanda's age. "A woman," Courtney remarked in a tone between surprise and admiration. "I'm sorry—I don't mean to be rude. But you're a woman, young and pretty... I'm not used..."

Amanda smiled. "It's all right. A lot of people are surprised." She raised a challenging eyebrow fleetingly at Cole. "And you're an electrician?" she said to Courtney. "I must say I feel the same surprise."

"I taught her everything she knows," Neil put in. "Now if I could just get her to work. Enough playing, you two," he said, waving his screwdriver at Cole and Courtney.

Courtney smiled beautifully at Cole. "Cole knows who the real worker is in this family."

I just bet he does, Amanda thought vehemently, quickly averting her face as heat rushed to her cheeks. After looking around, acting interested in a deliberately friendly manner, she left.

Obviously Courtney and Cole were very friendly, Amanda fumed, pulling a book from the shelf and plopping it on the desk. With swift, jerky movements she inserted a page into the typewriter. He was probably friendly with half the female population of the county. And obviously it was okay to be a capable female with brains, just not a minister. She placed her fingers on the keys of the typewriter, then realized she didn't even know what she was going to type.

She'd intended to work on her sermon. She certainly couldn't do that with her mind racing helter-skelter as it was. With a sigh she leaned back in the old chair. She had no right to feel so angry, so... so jealous, she thought, admitting to herself what she really felt. She was tired again, and utterly, totally, confused.

If she were interested in a relationship with a man—and she emphasized the word "if"—what in the world could she see in Cole Mattox? He was stubborn, a ladies man, obviously, and his morals—well, he apparently kissed women as easily as he shook hands.

It had been a stupid idea, she told herself. If Cole couldn't see her as she was or didn't want her as she was, there was no need to think more about it.

She took her things home to finish a sermon she never felt satisfied with. Then, in the afternoon, she went to visit

Mae, who appeared totally recovered, and later she went to Pa Hammond's. He kept her for dinner and for several hard-fought games of chess.

The day never did succeed in clearing and Amanda drove home through another evening closed in with misty rain. Her dark house looked exceedingly lonely. As she went up the back stairs, a sliver of alarm swept up Amanda's spine; the door was ajar.

Hesitantly she pushed it open. Surely she'd shut it tightly before leaving. She might not have bothered to lock it, but with the threat of rain, she had certainly shut it. She switched on the light; the kitchen was perfectly normal. Dropping her purse on the table, Amanda looked around and breathed easier. Everything appeared fine.

Feeling quite silly, but thinking it best to be cautious, Amanda looked through the rest of the small cottage, turning on lights as she went. Satisfied, she returned to the kitchen to make hot cocoa, but she'd still not bought any milk. Her gaze fell to the floor in front of the refrigerator. There was a footprint. It was faint, but definitely a footprint—and much too large to be her own. With her eyes widening and her heart picking up tempo, she followed the trail to the back door. There could be no doubt; someone with dirty shoes had tracked through her house.

She went back to the refrigerator. She knew she'd had a pound of bologna; it was gone. Apples? She wasn't sure. The bread? Two slices left. There'd been half a loaf at breakfast. Was someone stealing her food? Amanda couldn't believe it. Yet the evidence was there.

She recalled the car she'd seen that morning. Grabbing a flashlight and slinging on a raincoat, Amanda walked out the back door, playing the light across the deck and down the stairs. There were muddy footprints. She followed the impressions in the soft ground, but after two yards, they faded, though the trail did lead in the direction of the fence and the road to the abandoned farmhouse.

House? Amanda thought. It was more like a one-room chicken coop with every other slat missing. And trail? Half of what she'd seen could have been imagination. Still, if someone had stolen food—that part she was sure of—they might need help. She walked to the fence and gingerly climbed through the barbed wire. The black hulk of a car was visible beside the dilapidated shack at the top of the hill.

Flashlight playing on the dirt track in front of her, Amanda walked toward the car. It was damp, dark and dreary, and she thought she ought to have better sense. Yet, she wasn't frightened, and she took that to be a good sign.

She shone the light in the car window, coming unexpectedly upon the startled face of a boy, who was perhaps a very young sixteen. Startled herself, Amanda could do little but stare for a full ten seconds. She recognized him, had seen him at several of the church youth parties the past summer.

She motioned for him to roll down the window. "Ricky?" Her mind searched for the last name. "Ricky Leeds, isn't it?"

He nodded, his eyebrows drawn together, his jaw tight. Again they stared at one another. Amanda decided on the direct approach, her confidence spurred by a glance at the back seat: her half-gallon milk carton sat there next to a paper bag.

"Perhaps you've filled up on bologna, but I can offer you a cup of hot coffee on this dismal night," Amanda said matter-of-factly. The boy looked chagrined. "Come on down and tell me what's going on." She turned to go, as if sure he would follow, and was relieved when the car door opened. She waited and he fell into step just behind her. At the fence he held the barbed wire for her to go through.

Ricky Leeds was pitifully thin and pale. His dark-blond hair hung limp and dirty to his collar, and his blue eyes looked at Amanda warily.

Calmly Amanda filled the coffee maker. In seconds the aroma of the warm brew filled the room. Ricky twitched some, but Amanda took her time, saying little beyond, "Cream? Sugar? You missed the apple pie in here—it was shoved way back." But she allowed her instincts to listen closely. And then cautiously—afraid of frightening the boy, who was obviously in deep trouble—she began to question him.

Ricky related that his mother moved to Texas and left him behind. He was old enough now to take care of himself. His chin stuck out when he informed her of this point. He would be seventeen in December and would graduate in May. He'd been doing all right until the gas station where he'd been working shut down. After a week, he couldn't pay the rent on his room anymore. Now he was living in his car and going to school. "I'm going to graduate," Ricky concluded firmly. "Then I can get a good job. And I'd planned to pay you back when I could. All that I took was food. That's all."

"I know," Amanda said, covering the boy's hand with her own. He jerked his hand away. Her heart went out to him, but she shoved the emotions aside. Pity wasn't going to help Ricky. "Okay—so what you need now is a place to stay and a job." Unbidden, a thought struck Amanda.

"I'll find a place to stay once I get a job," Ricky said.

Amanda nodded. "You can stay here tonight. Maybe...I may know of someone who could use your help." She rose to clear the table and nearly bumped into Ricky as he came right behind her with the pie plates.

"I can stay out in my car," the boy said.

"No," Amanda said firmly. "I have a guest room—and a shower." The boy looked uncertain. "I'm offering you a helping hand, Rick."

Ricky nodded solemnly. "Okay."

Amanda grinned slightly. "You'd better get your car and any things you'll need."

She couldn't help looking in on him when she was sure he'd fallen asleep. He was curled beneath the covers and the moonlight played on his thin face. His hair, clean now, shimmered in the light. He's on the verge of manhood, Amanda thought, but still a child. How could his mother not care? She'd borne him, and yet... Amanda allowed the incomprehensible thought to pass. How could she know what had possessed the woman? How could she know her life? Ricky would be all right. He had it in him. He didn't seem resentful toward his mother or of the blows life had dealt him. He was ready to get on with the present and the future.

Later, in her own bed, Amanda thought of Paul Venard. He'd had hair like Ricky's. Her thoughts moved to Cole. The night they'd had dinner he'd mentioned needing a helper. It had been only one small comment; funny how it came back to her now. Cole was behind in two indoor remodeling jobs he'd promised to do before Christmas. Maybe Amanda could persuade him to take on Ricky. She didn't know how much Ricky knew about such things, but surely he could be a help.

Tomorrow was Saturday. She could drive over to Cole's ranch and talk to him. She'd not seen his place, but knew where the entrance to the driveway was. She squirmed at the whispered thought that this was a perfect opportunity to see Cole again.

In the morning, at five minutes after eight, Glenda Boyer breezed in Amanda's front door with a token preliminary

knock. Amanda started to her feet. She'd been talking with
Ricky—he, in the chair and she, curled up on the couch—
and sharing coffee and sweet rolls. She had been pleased to
see a great improvement in Ricky. They'd talked and
laughed. Amanda wore a cotton robe and fuzzy slippers.
Ricky wore jeans and a white T-shirt, his feet bare.

Glenda's gaze darted around the room, pausing noticeably at Ricky's feet, before returning to Amanda. Ricky
reddened and tossed back his fine hair. Amanda watched
Glenda's mouth open and close and could plainly see the
mean, petty thoughts whirling behind the astonished eyes
that were thoroughly taking in the friendly atmosphere, the
plate of half-eaten rolls, the coffee cups and the woman and
the young man who were plainly not dressed for company.

Chapter Eight

It was typical of Glenda Boyer to feel free to stop by at—Amanda pointedly looked at her watch—barely 8:05 on a Saturday morning. Shoving irritation aside, and trying to keep it there, Amanda greeted Glenda politely, making the introductions.

"Ricky is my houseguest for a day or two," she explained, smiling with slightly gritted teeth, and not about to explain further. Ricky was sullenly withdrawing again. The scene was embarrassing him, and Amanda's affairs were not any of Glenda's business. Actually Amanda would have preferred to let Glenda go on with her vicious thoughts. She even wanted to encourage them, then rebuked herself for the thought. A rumor would only hurt them all. She strove to act pleasant—and definitely innocent.

Ricky excused himself and went to the guest room. Glenda accepted an offer of coffee and Amanda went to the kitchen for another cup.

"That young man is not a member of our church, is he?" Glenda asked.

"Not an official member." Amanda smiled blandly and passed the cup of coffee to Glenda.

"Is he going to stay here long? It truly doesn't seem . . . well, you know."

"Yes, Glenda, I do know," Amanda replied, very pleasantly. "Don't worry about it. Now, what did you need to see me about this morning?"

"Oh, I . . . I needed to make sure of the date for the formal dedication of the new Sunday school rooms. Mary Hammond and Sarah Benton are helping me with the refreshments. A bit of planning does go into these things...." Glenda seemed to ramble on as the dry Buggy Creek rambled through the county. She explained the numerous plans, brought out a memo book and jotted down the date and several notes, all the while keeping an eye on the door to the guest room.

When she left, Amanda stood at the front door and waved goodbye. It was then she realized the real reason Glenda had stopped. Ricky's dilapidated Malibu was parked right behind the Jeep. Amanda hoped she could arrange a job and a place for Ricky to stay that day. Wagging tongues could burn like fire. And Ricky had been burned enough lately.

At midmorning Amanda left Ricky studying—the boy certainly seemed avid about it—and headed for Cole's. The clouds had parted, promising a blue sky. A fresh, fall breeze tugged at her hair. She didn't look too deeply into her emotions or consider why she wore designer jeans and a pale-yellow sweater and had left her hair floating to her shoulders. She didn't dare.

Stopping at Cole's driveway, she took a deep breath, downshifted and headed up the incline that wound its way through a deep fall-colored woods.

The drive was about three-quarters of a mile, opening into a clearing. A scruffy black and tan dog ran barking to greet her, its tail wagging furiously. On the right sat a small vacation trailer. Next to it was a large aluminum building, its wide doors open, revealing a workshop inside. Cole's truck was parked outside. On the left was the frame of what looked to be a two-story house. The back and sides of the first floor were built of concrete block, and set into the hill.

Amanda slid from the seat and bent to pet the dog, allowing him to sniff her legs fully before stepping away. Hearing Cole call, she turned to see him waving from the second floor of the house. She waved back. Her pulse quickened at the sight of his strong, wide-shouldered frame and his smooth, sure movements as he clambered down the ladder and strode to meet her. He wore a navy T-shirt, faded jeans and, as always when working, a carpenter's apron around his hips.

The dog bounced and wiggled, looking first at Cole and then at Amanda. "Some watchdog you have here," Amanda said as she stroked the dog's soft fur.

"I've taught him only to bite the bad ones. His name is Mac and he loves the ladies." His dark gaze was frankly curious.

"Like his master," Amanda quipped without thinking. Cole let it pass with a smile. She nodded toward the framework house. "Your house?"

"Yes—eventually. My brothers helped with the concrete, but since then it's just been me. I work on it weekends and some evenings."

"It's going to be quite a place. All southern exposure— passive solar heating?"

Cole nodded. "Yes. I'll have a small furnace, but plan to use it only to keep the pipes from freezing when I'm away. My heat will come from the sun and a wood stove." He spread his arm toward the trees. "I've plenty of fuel."

Amanda smiled. "It's beautiful here."

"Come on," he said, suddenly taking her hand. "I'll show you the house. You can see near to Anadarko from up there." Guiding her around the first floor he explained the room plan and the technique of laying concrete blocks. When Amanda commented that she'd worked on something similar in Mexico, he went into greater detail and she experienced a sense of pride at being able to meet him equally on his own terrain.

At the foot of the ladder Cole paused to lay aside his carpenter's apron. "Sorry—haven't built the stairs yet." He held the ladder while she climbed to the second floor and then came up behind her.

Amanda walked straight to one of the wide openings framed for a window. The view was breathtaking, and she gazed in delighted wonder, feeling as though the world were spread out before her. Cole stepped close.

"Like it?" he asked, his craggy voiced hushed.

Amanda nodded, allowing her gaze to roam over the vast panorama stretched before her. The rolling hills were clothed in flowing meadows and woods of sun-kissed trees. Here and there the golds and reds of fall were just beginning, but summer lingers in central Oklahoma. Looking farther west, she saw the blackened pastureland and remembered the night she'd met Cole.

He leaned close and pointed. "That red roof over there is my parents' house."

"How much of this is your family land?"

"Oh, nearly as far as you can see south and east, split between several uncles as well as my father." He took her hand, leading her to an east window. "This bit—to that line of trees— is my place. My father and I cleared this small acreage here when I was fifteen. This was to be my own." Cole pointed with one hand and kept hold of Amanda's hand with the other. She wondered why—and was so very glad he did.

"What's the steel building, your workshop?"

"That and storage for the lumber I use building this place and the others. And it's also for storing the things I keep collecting. As you can imagine, the trailer doesn't have much room." He pointed to rafters stacked neatly on the ground below. "I need my brothers again. Maybe tomorrow."

Amanda leaned her head against the window frame and relaxed. The sky was very blue above them. The sun illuminated the red highlights in Cole's hair, a light breeze teasing the strands that fell across his forehead. The world beyond seemed to sparkle like a fine diamond, none of its dirt and tragedy was visible from where they stood.

"Why did you become a minister?" Cole asked suddenly.

For a moment Amanda was taken off guard. His eyes searched hers, determined, yet revealing a faint confusion, as if he'd not meant to ask the question at all.

She smiled slightly, thinking: How can I explain? Will I sound foolish?

"I was drawn to it. It was something I felt I needed to do—something I could do—for my little corner of the world. Perhaps if you thought of why you went into carpentry, you'd understand. Like you, I was first taught at home. It was in my blood. The reasons really aren't so different from any that convince a person to do something."

Cole leaned his hands against the window frame and looked out. He nodded. "I think I can understand. When

I'm working with wood, it feels right, like I was meant to do this, like my body and my mind were made for it." He raised an eyebrow at her. "You come from a family of ministers?"

"My father and two of my three older brothers," Amanda said with a laugh. "The third brother is a car dealer over in Tulsa—very successful. You see, we Jamesons have a gift for gab."

Cole grinned, his teeth bright against his beard. "So you follow a family tradition?"

"Some," Amanda acknowledged a bit wryly. "For true family tradition I should have married a minister, not been one." Cole raised a questioning eyebrow. "At first," Amanda said, "it was difficult for my dad to understand. And he's a very understanding man—except when it came to his little girl. But we're all very close, so the family supported me, even though they couldn't quite comprehend my dreams."

He stared down at her from his greater height, his eyes warm. Amanda couldn't look away. His hand came up and gently stroked her cheek. She felt a magnetic tug toward him, but she didn't move. She enjoyed looking at him; his eyes reflected a warmth, a longing, and Amanda felt her body respond.

"My life has been quite different from yours, but my family equally understanding." Cole's voice was thoughtful. "I caused them all sorts of trouble—seems like from the time I was born. It was my dad who made explanations to the girl I left at the altar. Mom sent me boxes of cookies in the army and always extra money, too. I blew a lot on card games and just plain tearing around. Then when I couldn't seem to settle down, they still wrote, sent money, stayed in touch, never forcing me." His eyes searched hers. "Years ago, I used to go to that old church you preach in now." He grinned. "I threw pennies at the preacher when he had his eyes closed, praying—till Mom finally caught me."

The breeze touched his hair. Amanda listened to his words sadly. She knew he was trying to tell her he didn't fit with her. She wanted to touch him, to deny his words.

Abruptly Cole stepped away. "Did you come for something special, Pastor?" he asked, his eyes in that second turning cold and distant.

Pastor. Amanda felt as if he'd splashed ice water in her face. She was humiliated and angry at him for making her feel that way. She sought to gather her thoughts, to match Cole in his aloofness. "Yes... I need a favor."

"If I can." Cole led the way to the ladder. "Let's have something to drink...."

He was all smooth politeness. He held the ladder, careful not to touch Amanda as she descended. She felt she'd suddenly become diseased, untouchable. The air between them was so cool she shivered.

As they were walking toward his trailer, he said, "I can offer you a soft drink.... I don't have any wine." He half smiled. He was striving to remain distant, but he'd not forgotten.

Her heart gave a tug, and she grinned back. "A soft drink will be fine."

"Here." Cole pulled out two lawn chairs and sat them in front of the steps. "It's nicer outside—awfully cramped in here," he said, then ducked back into the trailer for their soft drinks.

Mac wiggled over and rested his nose on Amanda's thigh. She stroked his head and he closed his eyes in contentment. The sun was warm on her hair; it was quiet and peaceful. Hearing his movements in the trailer, Amanda thought about Cole—about his strength, his easy laughter, his kindness. He was an intelligent man. Why couldn't he see her as just Amanda Jameson? Why did he see some monstrosity of his imagination?

Cole returned with two cold soft drinks, handed her one and sat in the chair beside her.

"I have a sixteen-year-old boy who needs a job," Amanda began after a moment. "I remembered you said something about needing a helper. I don't know how much he knows about carpentry, but he's a determined worker and I hoped you'd... He's all alone," she ended self-consciously.

Cole didn't say anything for a minute. "Who is he?"

"His name is Ricky Leeds." She raised an eyebrow, wondering if Cole knew him. He shook his head. "I found him last night sleeping in his car," she said and went on to explain the situation. "Then Glenda Boyer stopped by this morning. Ricky and I had barely been up a half hour. We were having coffee and rolls and she walked in. There I was in my robe—Ricky barefoot. You can imagine what it looked like." She started to smile despite herself.

Cole grinned broadly. "I can imagine," he said, then drained the last of his drink. "Do you want me to give him a job and a home?"

"Oh no!" Amanda said hurriedly. "I think I have a perfect place for him. Pa Hammond needs someone and Ricky needs someone. They're both perfectly peevish, but I think they may be good for each other."

Cole looked at her thoughtfully. "Okay, Manda."

The coolness had slipped. Her heart fairly tripped over her ribs at his tone. He was looking at her, holding her gaze with his own. The magical connection popped and crackled between them. Nothing else mattered.

Then Cole's eyes broke away, his gaze going beyond her. Amanda detected the sound of an engine and a pickup pulled into the clearing. Tall, golden-haired Courtney Johnson waved as she slipped from the driver's seat. "Hello, you two." She swung a picnic basket on her arm, her smile for Cole.

Amanda talked to Pa Hammond. She reasoned and cajoled. When he finally gave in, she had the distinct feeling she'd been the one maneuvered. He looked forward to having Ricky, was excited in fact. Ricky reluctantly agreed—mostly to please her, Amanda suspected—but on a trial basis only. He wasn't going to put up with a grouchy old man. But at their first meeting, the two seemed to establish a kind of trust. Pa accepted Ricky as an equal, gave no quarter and asked for none. This did Ricky's pride a great deal of good.

And so that evening, Amanda was once again alone. Glenda Boyer called to make sure. So did Sarah Benton and Mae Loggin. "Glenda's been busy," Mae had said, with a chuckle. "I bet the whole county knows what she saw this morning—with a few embellishments."

The air was heavy and coolly humid. Amanda carried a warm cup of milk onto the back deck and stretched out in a lawn chair. The moon was full and grayly illuminated the cottony clouds as they floated past.

She was tired and her body felt bruised. For a while things had been almost gay at Pa Hammond's, with Ricky brightening by the moment. But now she was alone.

She kept remembering how she'd last seen Cole—in her rearview mirror, Courtney standing very close to him. Feeling quite out of place, Amanda had said goodbye soon after Courtney had appeared. Cole had given terse instructions for Ricky to come by Sunday afternoon and they'd work out a deal. Then Amanda had driven away. But she'd not been able to keep herself from glancing repeatedly in the rearview mirror. She'd almost hit a tree, in fact.

She grinned wryly, thinking how embarrassed she'd have been if she'd had an accident. What kind of excuse could she have given? I couldn't keep my eyes off you, so I ran into a tree?

The south wing was finished. Cole and Ricky had showed up late on a Friday afternoon "to do one finishing touch," Ricky had said with a grin.

Amanda was pleased with the changes she'd observed in Ricky. He was smiling quite a bit and had gained weight. She'd talked to several of his teachers and was confident the boy would qualify for one or more scholarships and go on to the university. He was dragging his feet in deciding if he wanted to, but then it was only early fall; school had only just begun.

Amanda couldn't begin to understand the relationship Ricky and Pa Hammond had formed. They seemed to bicker constantly, yet Ricky had brought Pa with him every day when he came after school to help Cole finish the painting. "Pa used to be a painter," Ricky explained. Cole even had Pa doing some of the easier trim work.

She'd seen very little of Cole for several weeks—by choice. She strove to put foolish thoughts behind her and immersed herself in her work. They were having a Sunday school drive, the children's Thanksgiving pageant loomed ahead and she'd taken on a weekly column in the local paper.

Closing up her office, she walked to the south wing. Cole and Ricky were atop ladders in the hall, Pa below, giving orders. "It's not even, boys. Make sure you get it all the way to the top."

"What is it?" Amanda asked curiously. It appeared they were adding wood molding to the top of the hall wall.

Ricky looked at Cole. He didn't say anything, just continued tapping the molding into place with his hammer. Even Pa shut his mouth, but his eyes danced.

Amanda followed the trim with her eyes. It went along the edge of the ceiling all down the hall on both sides. It was darkly stained oak, lovely against the white walls. As Amanda looked closer, she saw it was intricately and beautifully carved.

In wonder she turned back to Cole. He didn't look at her. Ricky grinned broadly. He couldn't resist. "Like it?"

"It's . . . beautiful."

They were done and Cole came slowly down the ladder. "I like to leave a piece of my own on everything I build."

"Cole taught me," Ricky said. "See, I did this section."

"It's beautiful," Amanda repeated.

"Nice piece of work, Cole. Real nice," Pa said. "Well, come on, Ricky. You're done for today. Get me on home."

"I'm coming—I'm coming." Pa limped ahead, while Ricky helped Cole gather the tools and ladders.

"Come on, Ricky!" Pa's raspy call came from the sanctuary.

Ricky rolled his eyes at Amanda and headed out of the hall.

"You've done well with him," Amanda said, as she walked with Cole.

"The boy's smart. He wants to learn."

"The trim . . . well, it's special. Thank you."

Cole shrugged. He was so close, yet so far away.

They stepped from the sanctuary and Amanda turned to make sure the doors had caught while Cole walked on to his truck. There was no reason for him to stop and talk. A pale-blue sedan pulled slowly into the churchyard, the tires crunching on the gravel. Amanda watched curiously as she slowly descended the steps.

A tall man emerged from the driver's seat and stood holding onto the car door, looking at her, the sun sparkling on his light hair.

Amanda's breath caught in the back of her throat.

Paul Venard.

At first she couldn't believe it. But yes, yes it was he. He was thinner than she remembered, his hair more neatly trimmed. In Mexico haircuts had been few and far between. He wore a light-blue knit shirt and tan slacks.

"Paul," she whispered, her pulse pounding in her ears. She didn't even notice her steps as she began running across the yard to meet him. "Paul!"

He held out both hands and grabbed hers in his. For a long moment they looked at one another. He'd aged some, not much, perhaps there was more silver in his blond hair, but he looked far younger than forty-five. The same winning smile touched his lips; the same dancing light shone in his blue eyes. The sun was bright upon his silky hair. He pulled Amanda to him, and they hugged each other. Then he held her away again.

"Let me look at you, Amanda," Paul said, his gaze running over her face.

She laughed up at him. "You, too!" Her vision was blurred by tears.

Paul wiped her tears away with his thumb. "You've changed."

She inclined her head. "Have I?" The question was breathless.

"Yes." Paul spoke softly. "More of a woman."

Watching Amanda and the tall stranger, Cole felt the hair stand on the back of his neck.

"Gee..." Ricky stared unabashed. "Who's that?"

Cole shrugged, then turned and hoisted the ladder into the pickup. "Get that stuff stowed, Ricky," he said shortly. The boy did as he was told, halfway looking over his shoulder at Amanda.

Pa Hammond leaned against the side of the truck, taking the weight off his bad leg. "Looks like Amanda knows that feller pretty good."

It sure did, Cole thought, taking his time arranging the tools, refusing to turn around.

Ricky finished and started for his car. "Ready, Pa?"

Nodding, Pa started after him. He paused near Cole. "You're being mighty foolish when it comes to that woman, boy," he said in a low knowing voice.

Cole glanced up quickly, but Pa simply limped on after Ricky. Cole's gaze strayed to the couple, who were now slipping into the blue sedan. The man with Amanda was tall, slim and handsome.

Chapter Nine

With Paul's guiding hand on her elbow, Amanda slipped into the car seat. Her eyes strayed up the slight hill to where Ricky was just turning his car around and then to Cole, who stood leaning against the tailgate of his truck.

Cole. She'd forgotten him. The sun glinted off his dark hair and he looked her way, but he was too distant for her to see his expression. What must he think?

She glanced at Paul, and he smiled warmly. Amanda's heart sped, her mind whirling with a million questions. What was Paul doing now? Where had he been? And above all, why was he here?

The questions burned her tongue, clamoring to be asked, but she remained quiet. She wanted to simply enjoy this moment of seeing a friend, a very dear friend.

"Sit down," she said, tossing her purse to the table as they entered her house. "I'll make us some coffee."

She was glad Paul didn't follow her to the kitchen. She needed a minute to catch her breath and straighten her thoughts. And he seemed to need a minute, too. With trembling hands, Amanda filled the glass pot of the coffee maker. Excited and numb from shock at the same time, she struggled to sort out her emotions. Why hadn't he called? To just show up...

She smiled, thinking of Cole seeing them together. Could he possibly have been jealous? That's a petty thought, Manda, she scolded. What did she care anyway what Cole Mattox thought?

She carried the tray of coffee and cups into the living room, setting it on the table in front of the couch. Paul was looking at books on the shelf. He turned to watch her. His blue eyes were as bright as she remembered. But he was different, of course. No one stays the same. And she felt different too. For a fleeting moment Paul surveyed her gently, almost sadly.

"It's good to see you, Amanda." His accent was softer than she remembered, less noticeable. And she suddenly realized he'd never shortened her name to Manda, or Mandy.

"You, too."

He leaned a hand on the back of a nearby chair. His other hand flexed nervously. "I'm sorry I didn't call first. Cowardice on my part. I was afraid you wouldn't want to see me." His gaze held a question.

She looked at him and smiled softly. "It doesn't matter. I'm glad you came."

His face relaxed a fraction. "Mira told me you were here. Talking with her was the first I'd really heard about you."

"You could have written, Paul."

He smiled gently. "I felt it was best I didn't." He drank his coffee. "I was a pretty confused man, Amanda. I wanted to write—started half a dozen letters, but they all ended up sounding as muddled as I felt." He gave a sound somewhere between a sigh and a laugh. "Midlife crisis, I believe they call it." He looked at her. "I'd call it wanting to live two ways at once. I did want you, Amanda, but another part of me wanted the kind of life that had no room for a wife or for children. And you were too young to settle for less. And I guess I still carry Laura with me...perhaps I always will, even though she's been gone all these years. I guess I've become an old widower, stuck in his ways."

Amanda touched his hand. "You don't have to explain."

"I know. I couldn't possibly explain it all, but I just needed to tell you some of this. Amanda...I needed very much to see you—to apologize, for one thing. It was brutal cutting out on you like I did years ago. We...I..." He paused and looked intent. "I guess I need to settle things of the past so I can get on with the future."

They looked at each other for a long while. Paul was her friend. That was all that could ever be between them. Amanda knew it in her heart. She never, ever could have felt for Paul what she felt for Cole. Cole... Even now she thought of him. Cole's eyes were dark. Why was it that even as she looked into Paul's pale, gentle eyes, her mind pictured the soft, coffee-colored eyes of a man with brown velvety hair and a rhythm to his walk? A man who could warm her blood with his glance?

Would it always be this way for her? Would it never be the right man, the right time?

She pushed the thoughts aside. "Tell me everything," Amanda demanded brightly. "Where are you going now? Have you been traveling? Have you seen anyone else we used to know? And how did you find me anyway?"

Paul laughed. "Tall order, Amanda. Do you have a couple of days to listen?" he teased.

"No, but I do have all evening. Stay for dinner and I'll cook you a mean plate of scrambled eggs—and I have fresh pie made from apples off the tree right outside my back door."

Paul's tone matched Amanda's for briskness. "You have a deal. First question—I'm on my way to California to a job as managing advisor of Corbin, Incorporated."

"Oh, I've heard of it." Amanda freshened their coffee. "They teach successful business practices overseas, don't they?"

Paul nodded. "Yes, in order to feed people, in what they term practical, long-term ways." He went on to explain his job, his face reflecting the same intense vitality Amanda remembered from years ago. But there was now an added look of peacefulness to his features. He'd found what he had been searching for.

Paul paused and Amanda realized she'd not truly been listening. She'd been thinking of Cole and of the unrest in her own life.

They went through one pot of coffee and Amanda made another. Dusk was falling. Amanda scrambled eggs while Paul made toast and they talked almost nonstop. Paul told of his depression, which had come and gone through the past years, of Paris in spring and winter, of beginning to paint—"compulsively," Paul said. Painting released emotions and helped him think. The only old friends he'd seen were Mira Shaw and Teddy Coffey, both in Paris. But he'd made a new friend, a manager for Corbin's in France, and through him had become involved in the organization. When he'd decided to take the job, he knew he had to see Amanda, and Bishop Henderson had told him where she was.

"Hey, enough of me," Paul said, as they again settled on the couch with their after-dinner pie and coffee. "Your turn now. What happened after I left Mexico? And how did you get here? And how are you doing?'' His blue eyes looked at her warmly as he copied the rapid-fire questions she'd asked before.

Amanda laughed, kicked off her shoes and curled her feet beneath her. She told him of new friends, of why and how she came to Coogan and of her life since. When she touched briefly on her restlessness, she saw understanding in his eyes. She said nothing about her feelings for Cole or about the new longing for a lifetime mate. It would perhaps distress Paul. Dusk turned to pitch-black night. Neither of them noticed the passing hours; two years was a long time to cover.

Restless, Cole switched off the television and on impulse, decided to drive over to the Johnsons'. Courtney lived with her brother, Neil, and his wife. They all sat around talking for a while, then Cole decided he couldn't stand sitting any more.

''Want to drive over to Chickasha for a movie?'' he asked Courtney. ''We could still make the second show.''

''Sure.'' Courtney smiled. Neil and his wife smiled too. It made Cole uncomfortable.

He took the road that led past the church and the parsonage. Quickest way, he told himself. The pale-blue sedan sat in front of the parsonage. The porch was dark, lights shone cozily from the living room. Cole checked his watch: nearly eight o'clock.

''Want some popcorn or candy?'' Cole asked Courtney in the lobby of the theater.

''Just a Coke,'' Courtney said. ''Have to watch my weight.''

Cole grinned. ''Looks great to me.''

Courtney smiled a sexy kind of smile. She was fun to be with, intelligent, too. But her smile didn't make him feel the way Amanda's did. Damn that woman! Her face kept popping into his mind. And what was that guy still doing there?

Cole found he couldn't keep his mind on the movie. Restlessly he squirmed in his seat, impatient for the show to be over. Courtney looked at him several times from beneath her long lashes.

It was well after eleven when they drove home past the parsonage. The blue sedan was still there; lights still shone cozily from the living room windows.

At the last minute, Cole turned the steering wheel, pulling into the parsonage driveway.

Courtney raised her eyes to him.

"Just thought of something I need to ask Pastor Jameson," Cole said, feeling foolish and angry at the same time. "I'll only be a minute."

He expected Courtney to wait in the truck, but she hopped down and followed.

Rapid footsteps on the porch, followed closely by loud knocking on the front door, startled Amanda and Paul. They had been in such deep conversation that neither had seen lights or heard a car drive up. Amanda's thoughts flew as she looked at Paul. All she could think of was Glenda Boyer. What would this look like? And for heaven's sake, the clock showed nearly eleven- thirty. The time had flown!

With a puzzled look at Paul, Amanda hurriedly padded across the room in her stocking feet. Her mind raced, thinking there could be some emergency.

Opening the door, Amanda's gaze first contacted a wide male chest, denim jacket hanging open. She looked up, greatly surprised, into Cole's brown eyes. They were fuming.

"What's wrong?" Amanda's gaze ran past Cole to Courtney, who stood at his elbow. "Is it Ricky? Pa?"

"No...no, nothing like that." Cole's voice was low. "We were just passing. I saw your lights on and thought of something I needed to ask you about."

Puzzled, Amanda moved back as Cole pushed his big frame into the living room. "Come in," she said, though he already was. "Hello, Courtney." She couldn't quite think what to say or do. Never had she expected it to be Cole at the door. And he was acting so bullish. What in the world could it be? Her heart gave an unexpected pang at seeing him with Courtney.

Paul rose from the couch. "Oh...Paul, I'd like you to meet Cole Mattox," Amanda said as Paul stepped forward, shaking hands easily with Cole. Paul stood slightly taller than Cole, leaner, more finely drawn. Cole smiled tightly. Amanda sensed his tension—or was it her own? "This is an old friend, Paul Venard."

"How do you do, Mr. Mattox," Paul said politely, his eyes studying Cole.

"Hello," Cole said gruffly, sizing up Paul in return.

"And this is Courtney Johnson," Amanda continued. Paul took Courtney's hand and the young woman nodded a hello. "Cole built the new wing of the church, and Courtney did some of the electrical work." Uneasily Amanda saw how cozy her living room looked, with the flickering fire, the dirty dessert dishes, empty coffeepot and cups on the table in front of the couch. How did she manage to get into these situations that looked like...oh, like so much more? Cole's gaze rested on her hotly. "You wanted to ask me something?" She spoke very pointedly.

Taking her almost roughly by the elbow, Cole ushered her toward the kitchen. "Yes," he said. "It'll just take a minute," he tossed over his shoulder to Courtney and Paul, who stood in the middle of the living room looking at each other, bewildered.

Cole practically threw Amanda into the kitchen. Automatically he flipped on the overhead light. The swinging door bounced several times behind them. Cole towered over her, his eyes hard, his dark hair and beard shiny in the bright light.

"What is this all about?" Amanda demanded. She felt like David facing Goliath, but her temper was her strength.

"You're entertaining a man in your home—alone—at eleven-thirty at night," Cole hissed, his gravelly voice a loud whisper.

Amanda stared at him. She couldn't believe it! He was practically accusing her of... well, she wasn't sure of what, but he didn't make it sound nice. "Of all the ugly innuendos!" she hissed back, fuming, looking for words. "Paul is an old friend who stopped to see me. We haven't seen each other in years, so we got to talking. We never realized the time." Backing up, she raised her hands and then dropped them, shaking her head. "Why am I explaining this to you? You're warped, you know that?"

A whisper in the back of her brain said a minister shouldn't talk like that. But she didn't feel like a minister at the moment. She was a woman speaking to a hardheaded man. And he was out with another woman—another beautiful woman!

"He must be a close friend, the way you two greeted each other at the church this afternoon."

Amanda tapped her foot. "How do you greet Courtney?" Her voice was low, each word said precisely.

Cole glared back. "That's not the point. You two," he said, pointing his finger, "have to observe proprieties. What will people think? How's it going to look? Glenda Boyer thought she had fun with you and Ricky. What would she say to this?''

Amanda looked at Cole through a red mist of hot anger. ''I don't particularly care.''

''Well, you should. You should at least try acting a little more like a proper minister.''

''And what are your rules for the way a proper minister should act, Mr. Mattox?'' Amanda no longer attempted to whisper.

''Keep your voice down,'' Cole hissed.

''Is that one of the rules?'' Amanda goaded. Cole advanced. ''I thought 'Love thy neighbor' should come first.''

Suddenly Cole was very close. A breathless eternity hung between them, Amanda exceedingly aware of his warmth and the powerful energy that flowed between them.

The next second his hands gripped her upper arms and he pulled her to him, his lips pressing hard on her own. Surprised, Amanda didn't resist. A split second later she was responding, fire burning up from deep within, spreading like hot lava throughout her body.

After an eternity, Cole raised his head. Amanda's lips felt bruised and swollen and she couldn't take her eyes from his. Slowly Cole's warm, confused gaze flowed over her face and stopped at her lips. With a tender motion, as if touching fine china, he stroked them with his thumb. Then very slowly, almost reverently, he lowered his lips to hers and kissed her. A true, warm, loving, exquisitely powerful kiss.

When he lifted his head and his eyes looked into hers, Amanda saw anguish and confusion in their brown depths. Her heart melted, going out to him. He released her and turned away. A great breath shook his body. ''I'm sorry,'' he said, then walked from the room.

Standing with her arm outstretched to where he had stood, Amanda watched through a blur of tears as the white enamel door swung back and forth. She turned and clutched the sink. There was a murmur of voices in the living room, then the sound of the front door closing. A few seconds later, the kitchen door squeaked open.

"Amanda?" Paul's voice was very quiet. Amanda couldn't even hear his steps toward her. He touched her shoulder, concern ringing in his voice. "Amanda?"

She managed a nod. "I'm okay." But she didn't want him to see her face. Sensing this, Paul moved to sit at the table. Amanda splashed cold water on her face and dried it slowly with the towel.

"Oh, he makes me so mad!" she said at last.

"He was jealous of me," Paul said, watching her carefully when she turned around.

"Ha! He just likes to run other people's lives, telling them how they should act."

"He was jealous," Paul repeated as if to himself. He grinned sadly.

Cole held himself in tight control. Without a word, he nodded politely to Venard, took a puzzled Courtney by the elbow and escorted her out the door. Still not saying anything, he helped her into the truck, got in beside her and slammed the door. He swore under his breath. The man was French! And tall, blond and suave. Amanda didn't have a chance. His mind blazed with visions of her face, of her crimson lips. Feelings raged within him that he didn't want to recognize: love, jealousy and burning desire.

And anger at himself. He'd acted a fool. He knew perfectly well their argument hadn't been about what a minister should look and act like. Amanda knew it too. The fact was, he was crazy about her and didn't want to be. He simply would not be!

Groaning inwardly, he remembered her face. Still, he could still see her lips, swollen from the force of his own, and the hurt in her eyes.

He drove almost blindly, his unconscious mind taking over on a road he knew by heart. Courtney's quiet voice drew him back.

"You're being a fool," she said.

"What?" he managed, his mind still whirling.

"You're being a big, dumb blockhead."

"So I've been told," Cole replied, his mind going back to Pa's words of the afternoon.

"Well, you need to be told again. You're acting as stupid as a cat with a stick tied to its tail. She likes you, and you're crazy about her. Yet you seem determined to screw it all up."

"I am not!" Cole denied vehemently. "She's a minister, for crying out loud!"

"She's a woman," Courtney stated firmly.

Cole sighed. She was that, he admitted silently to himself. Finally.

Amanda walked Paul to his car.

"I'll write," he said.

"Me too."

"It will work out between you and Cole," Paul said gently.

Amanda looked at him sadly and shook her head.

"It will; I know it will. Amanda, you were meant to marry, to have a family of your own. I wish..." He let it go.

Later, Amanda lay in bed feeling strangely empty. Today had been too much. First the overwhelming surprise of seeing Paul again... and then Cole.

Cole. Her spirit fairly breathed the name. Thoughts of him overshadowed everything. "Oh, that man!" she whispered aloud and punched her pillow. Such a bullheaded man! Barging in—embarrassing her, telling her how she should live. What gave him the right to set rules and to judge her? She couldn't possibly care for such a man. It was ridiculous! Imagine herself, always thinking—daydreaming, for heaven's sake—of him. It was totally laughable. They had practically nothing in common. He was...

A tear slid down her cheek, for she recalled the determination with which he'd fought the fire that night months ago, the tender look in his eyes when he'd helped Mae that afternoon she fell, the skill of his hands when he'd put up the special trim for the south wing and the patience in his voice when he instructed Ricky.

And she remembered the way his lips burned onto hers, the way he made her body come alive.

"Oh!" she breathed aloud as she punched her pillow again and tried to toss aside the memories. He couldn't see her! Not as a woman!

She lay very still as a thought formed. Perhaps he had tonight—he'd definitely been concerned at her being alone with Paul. He'd only be concerned like that if he saw her as a woman... with a man. Could it be?

A week slipped by. In her heart, Amanda expected Cole to contact her, though consciously she dismissed the thought as so much nonsense. She didn't care to see him anyway, not after their last confrontation, she told herself. And, at the dedication ceremonies for the south wing, she fumed at herself even as she scanned every face, looking for the familiar dark beard and chocolate-colored eyes. He hadn't come. Well, he could at least call or come by to apologize for his outlandish behavior that night, couldn't he? But he didn't.

She saw his sleek black truck a few times from a distance. That was all.

Well, she wasn't about to contact him. At first it was out of wounded pride, but after she'd calmed down, she still wouldn't be the one to call or go by. He'd made it plain he wanted nothing to do with her. She had to accept that. She couldn't bear any more rejection. The whole situation was probably awkward for Cole, as well, and she didn't want to make it any worse for him.

She toyed with the idea of leaving. It was so hard to stay in Coogan, knowing Cole was so very near. She hated the thought of running into him when he was with another woman. Jealousy was an ugly, hurtful thing. Several times she actually picked up the phone to call Bishop Henderson, but each time she changed her mind. Finally she decided she simply couldn't leave. She simply couldn't run away from the problem. There was nowhere to run that the longings in her heart wouldn't follow.

The weeks passed. Fall became winter. Amanda succeeded, somewhat, in pushing thoughts of Cole to the back of her mind and tried to close the door on the whole affair.

But the door wouldn't stay closed. It opened a crack every time she saw his truck or the sun glinting on his dark hair. And Ricky told her a great deal about Cole: Cole could build anything, or if Cole Mattox couldn't build it, then it simply couldn't be built. Cole had a new band saw. Cole was adding a spa to Neil Johnson's house. The roof was on Cole's house now. Ricky had helped. Cole had a date with a real foxy blonde from the city.

Even Pa Hammond enjoyed speaking about Cole every chance he got. Or was it just that she listened more avidly whenever Cole's name was mentioned?

One late-November day, as Amanda was coming out of Coogan Grocery and Cole was going in, they bumped right into each other.

Amanda's grocery bag slipped from her arms, and Cole quickly reached out his strong hands to steady her. She stared into Cole's brown eyes, for that brief moment, forgetting where they were and ignoring the frigid air gusting around them, aware only of his scent, of the aura of strength about him. Her heart throbbed. He was so close; she longed to touch his soft beard.

Cole broke the gaze and bent to pick up the things spilled from her sack.

"Oh, I'm sorry," Amanda said, flustered. "I just wasn't looking."

Cole nodded. Another pair of hands pitched in, retrieving a rolled-away can of soup. Amanda looked into Billy's smiling face.

"Hello, Amanda." His eyes twinkled.

"Well, hello, Billy."

She rose and Cole carefully placed the sack in her arms. "How have you been, Amanda?" he asked, regarding her calmly.

"...Fine. Just fine. The new wing on the church is working out well. We all thank you for the good job." She wanted to say: I miss you. I think of you. I long for you.

"I'm glad everyone's pleased. Well..." He nodded toward the grocery store.

"Goodbye," Amanda said, turning quickly and moving toward the Jeep, not wanting him to see the hurt she feared was written all over her face.

Billy came behind her, opening the door for her. "Amanda, I understand you and Cole...that you're not seeing him. How about going out with me? Would you like to go to dinner? To a show?"

He shoved his hands in his pockets and gave a boyish, expectant smile. She had to smile back. "Thank you so much, Billy. I can't tell you how much. But no, I think it's best not.''

Billy shrugged good-naturedly. ''Can't blame a guy for trying.'' He waved and backed quickly toward the store.

The weeks marched on, one after another. The church membership grew steadily, especially with young people. There were numerous parties and dinners, weddings and a few funerals. Also, Amanda found herself doing much more counseling, wondering always if her guidance could be in the least helpful when she herself had so many questions about her own life.

Lowry filled in for her one Sunday, and Amanda went home to visit her parents for a week. When she returned she noticed green buds beginning on the trees and was actually surprised. Spring was coming and she'd not even noticed.

Chapter Ten

Cole struggled into his tight-fitting dress boots, wondering why in the world he'd accepted Mae Loggin's invitation anyway. She was throwing what she called her annual spring wingding. That this was the first year she'd had it, didn't bother Mae. She said everyone needed a party to wake up from the winter blahs, and she intended to have one every year from now on.

An inner voice whispered: because Mae mentioned Amanda Jameson was going to be there, that's why you're going.

He shrugged into his shirt, then bent to roll the window of his trailer out wider. The weather was unseasonably warm. They'd been having plenty of spring rain this year, but not today. Today the sun was bright in a clear sky—as if Mae had ordered it from above, Cole chuckled to himself. Mae was a rather persuasive woman.

Cole glanced at his house. He liked to look at it, remembering when the space had been occupied solely by rugged, red clay earth. Now a two-story, rock and cedar shingled home stood there. Cedar had been Amanda's suggestion; it was her favorite.

He planned to move into the house within the next few weeks, though much work remained to be done on the interior. The outside was totally completed, thanks largely to Ricky Leeds. The boy had a natural aptitude for carpentry and was now considering attending a local community college, so he could still work and train under Cole. Cole was glad; he liked the boy, even though it seemed every other word out of Ricky's mouth had to do with one Amanda Jameson. Cole had the sneaking suspicion Ricky did it on purpose.

Amanda went to the State Fair with Dan Cooper. Amanda and Dan Cooper had dinner with Pa and Ricky. Amanda and Dan Cooper hosted a teen dance. Amanda and Dan...

Cole had seen this Dan Cooper. He had prematurely gray hair.

Cole passed the church on his way to the Loggin's home. The staunch white building reminded him of Amanda: sturdy, but with fine lines. She fit there. He'd seen her. Twice the past winter he'd sneaked into Sunday services without her ever being aware of his presence.

Amanda Jameson was quite a woman, Cole thought. No denying it. He looked with puzzlement within himself. He'd tried hard at first to convince her he wasn't the man for her, and now, when she apparently had come to the same conclusion, he didn't like it. He wished...oh, hell, he didn't know what he wished.

The wide back porch stretching the length of the Loggins' home, blazed with Mae's colorful pots of mums and daffodils. Tables, heavily laden with food, lined the length of the railing at one end of the porch. A country band tuned

their instruments on a raised platform in the yard. Nearby
was a larger wood deck set up for dancing. Numerous picnic tables dotted the lawn.

People milled in and out of the house. Most of Coogan
had turned out, Cole guessed. Spotting his own parents and
his youngest brother, Billy, with his date, he waved. He
didn't see Amanda.

In the large kitchen Mae greeted him warmly, gave him a
glass of Lowry's homemade wine and indicated the table
with serve-yourself punch and soft drinks, then whirled off
to tend to other guests. Cole sipped his glass and, over the
rim, saw Amanda enter the kitchen. Standing unobserved
against a back wall, he allowed himself to simply look at
her.

Her honey-brown hair swirled up in a loose knot, stray
wisps brushing her face. Her skin was creamy, and for a
moment, Cole remembered how soft and smooth it felt. She
wore a dark-green skirt decorated with Indian embroidery
and a matching silky blouse that highlighted her luminous
green eyes.

The next point struck Cole rather hard—she wasn't alone.

Laughing, Amanda held the hand of Dan Cooper, pulling him into the room to greet Mae. The man was of me-
dium height, stocky and well built, with silver-gray hair,
though he couldn't be much older than Amanda. Cole felt
an ache and recognized it for what it was: jealousy.

A few seconds later his eyes locked with Amanda's as she
looked beyond Mae and spotted him. Even with the large
country kitchen between them and other people milling
about, Cole felt the energy touch him. It pitted in his stomach, then trailed up to tense his shoulders. He could almost
feel her lips on his, her energy vibrating within his arms.

The ache within him grew, and he had to get out of her
sight. Nodding imperceptibly, keeping his face impassive,

Cole turned and walked through to the living room and out the front door. Obviously the Preacher had brought a date, he told himself as he stood on the front porch. The thought irritated him immensely.

Amanda had played upon the edges of his mind a lot since that night months ago when he'd made such a fool of himself. He'd only seen her a few times since—but he was vitally aware of her existence anyway. When he'd bumped into her that time in the grocery store, he'd almost apologized for bursting in on her and Paul Venard. He owed her that. But with Billy looking on . . . And he didn't know how to say it. A hundred times during the winter, he'd started to call, to apologize, to talk to her. And then those two times in the church, when he'd not been able to face her. He'd held back, not really knowing why, just that he felt unsure of himself. What could he offer her? When his mind drew up full pictures, he couldn't quite see himself as the boyfriend, the lover, or the husband of a minister.

Hell, how he ached for her. Cole looked down and realized he was squeezing his glass. He considered leaving, but changed his mind. Maybe he would get a chance to dance with Amanda. He hedged on the thought, telling himself he was being a pure fool. But what would one dance hurt?

It was the first time in months Amanda had been this close to Cole. Close? her mind ridiculed. He was at the far end of the giant kitchen with a least eight people and a table between them. But it was as if he touched her when he looked at her. Amanda's mouth felt dry as she pulled her gaze from Cole's back as he walked from the kitchen. Mae offered Amanda and Dan a taste of Lowry's wine. "He's mighty proud of it," she said. Then after the wine, they got themselves tall glasses of cool punch.

After commenting to Mae on the perfection of the weather for the party, Amanda led Dan out onto the porch.

"Looks like the whole county is here," Dan commented.

"Half of it at least," Amanda chuckled. Her eyes met Dan's and she flushed under his warm gaze.

Dan Cooper, veterinarian, was thirty-one, a widower with one small boy, and a very nice man. He'd moved to Coogan in January, and he and Amanda had spent a great deal of time together right from the start, though they'd only actually begun to date in the past few weeks. But all along, Amanda had been fully aware that in no way did Dan make her feel as Cole Mattox did. She hadn't forgotten Cole. She remembered his kiss as if it'd just been yesterday.

Her eyes strayed quite often that afternoon, looking for the shiny dark hair, her ears listening for the sound of the familiar gruff drawl. She saw Cole several times: once with his parents, once dancing with a pretty blonde, and another time with Courtney, and still another time talking earnestly with Mae. They looked toward her and Amanda looked away quickly. What were they talking about? Why was Cole scowling?

Dan whirled her around on the plywood dance floor that had been temporarily erected in the backyard. The music ended and they moved onto the lawn near some bushes that bordered the porch.

"Wait here," Dan said. "I'll get us something to drink."

"Thanks." Amanda smiled lightly and attempted to catch her breath. "I could sure use it."

The music began again, and Amanda tapped her foot to the beat as she watched dancers whirling around the platform. Glenda Boyer tripped heavily by with her husband and waved to Amanda. She'd formed an understanding with Glenda over the past months—Amanda wasn't quite sure how, but was glad for it. They accepted each other.

Pa Hammond was talking brightly to petite and elderly Evie Moore. Their relationship was looking romantic, and a scandalous rumor circulated that Pa had even spent the night at Evie's house. Roy had had a fit, and wanted Amanda to talk to his father, but Amanda said she doubted she could tell Pa anything he didn't know.

Ricky held hands with Paula Bond, his feelings clearly written on his thin, plain face. Todd Walker glowered at Amanda from a picnic table nearby. He thought it unseemly, her dancing. There'd been several raised eyebrows, probably more than Amanda had seen, but all in all she felt more at home than ever before. She'd been in Coogan over a year now and had shared life with these people—their concerns, their joys and sorrows, even their dangers. They were her friends.

A voice spoke from near her shoulder. "Care to dance, Amanda?" It was a deep, gruff voice, and turning, Amanda looked into familiar cocoa-colored eyes. Cole held out his hand. Without speaking, she slowly put her hand in his. At his touch, a slight tremor weaved up her arm. Feeling her face flush, Amanda tore her gaze from his.

Together they stepped up on the platform. Cole's hand was warm upon her back as he whirled her around. Awareness of anything but him and his nearness slipped from her mind. She looked into the blue-plaid pattern of his shirt, her senses picking up the warm sweet scent of his after-shave. It was familiar, wonderfully familiar. And she admitted honestly to herself that she'd desperately wanted him to approach her and had prayed he would. Her heart soared.

The music changed to a slower beat. Cole managed to put his head nearer her ear while still keeping an ultrarespectable distance between their bodies.

"You're having a good time, Miss Amanda?" he asked in a husky whisper.

"Yes, thank you," Amanda said politely, cooly. She was so aware of him she couldn't believe it—his breath touching her temple, the barely perceptible throb of pulse in his neck, the roughness of his callused palm as he held her hand—of everything about him.

"I think I owe you an apology."

Her gaze shot up to his. "Yes."

He grinned slightly. "I apologize."

Amanda fought back a smile. How could he melt her this way? "Accepted."

The music ended and Cole led Amanda from the dance floor. Her heart dipped. She didn't want him to go.

They walked back beside the porch where Dan stood waiting with two glasses of punch. Amanda made the introductions, feeling somewhat ill at ease as she watched the two obviously sizing up one another like a pair of roosters. Cole was the epitome of politeness, shaking Dan's hand, speaking lightly. Then he turned and left.

It was dark when Dan saw her home. He kissed her forehead lightly. When she turned to go in, he stopped her. "Amanda..." His hands on her shoulders, Dan turned her around, and she looked up into his earnest face. "I..." he began, then lowered his lips to kiss her.

Watching his lips descend, Amanda turned her face. She just couldn't kiss him. *She just couldn't*. It was a lie, all a lie. No matter how much she'd tried in the past months to dismiss, to deny, her feelings for Cole Mattox, to place those feelings with Dan Cooper, she'd not succeeded. She couldn't go on pretending to herself or to Dan that they could have any sort of relationship beyond that of friendship.

"Oh, Dan, I'm sorry. I..." Her eyes misted as she searched his gentle face.

He looked at her for a long minute. "I care for you, Amanda." Dan's voice was husky with sadness. He sensed what Amanda left unsaid. She had to force herself to look fully at his face.

His eyes hardened with determination. "I don't give up easily, Amanda."

She smiled in spite of herself. Then she had to stop her lips from quivering. "I'm sorry, Dan," she said firmly. "There's nothing to give up on."

He scowled, his eyes hard and stubborn. "We'll see." He pivoted and stalked to his car.

Amanda watched him, her heart heavy. She'd hurt him.

She raised her eyes toward the deep blackness that was the Hammond pasture beyond the church, and saw again Cole's face as she'd sat upon his lap that night he'd pulled her from the fire.

Would she never forget Cole? Amanda wondered as she lay in bed. Would he always be there, but not for her? She turned her face to the pillow and cried. After a few minutes, she sniffed, reached for a tissue and blew her nose. He'd approached her this evening; he'd apologized. Did it mean anything at all?

Amanda had expected Cole to contact her after that evening, but the days went by and he never called, never sought her out. A thousand times, she toyed with the idea of marching over to his place and telling him just what she thought. He was a stubborn man! But she wouldn't let him see how much she cared. She wouldn't put him on the spot like that—nor herself, either, for that matter. She'd feel a fool chasing after him that way. Either he was interested, or he wasn't.

She couldn't quite believe he wasn't. The magical feeling had still vibrated between them that evening at Mae's, even after all those weeks that had seemed so long—weeks when she thought she'd forgotten him, only to have his image pop into her mind, or only to catch a glimpse of him, and have her heart start racing.

Willing her fingers to be patient, Amanda worked to slip the stems of early spring Shasta daisies into the weave of the picnic basket. She was out of sorts and trying to rise above it for the busy day ahead. It was the day of the Ladies Club's Annual Spring Event and Box Social. The sale of crafts and baked goods would begin in the morning, and at noon several quilts would go up for auction. Then the box social would begin.

Twenty-eight females, from thirteen-year-old Jill Davis on up to Evie Moore, had agreed to take part and would be bringing elaborate picnic lunches in gaily decorated boxes or baskets, to be offered at auction to the highest male bidder. Then the woman who had made the lunch and the buyer would go off and have lunch together.

Tradition maintained that the ownership of the lunches be kept secret. Every man was to take a chance on whom he'd end up eating with—as well as what he'd be eating. But also by tradition, the men managed, discreetly of course, to find out whose box was whose.

Amanda groaned inwardly, thinking of it. She had tried to beg off—after all, she was the minister. That excuse hadn't washed. "You're a woman of this church," Mae Loggin had maintained, grinning like a cat the whole while. "It's your duty to help raise money."

But to have her basket go up for auction—who would want to bid on it and eat lunch with the minister? Dan, of course. He was the only available and interested man around. She'd tried to make it clear to him that there was no future for them. But he'd still asked her out, and she'd declined. But she was beginning to see that Dan Cooper was indeed a very stubborn man.

People came from miles away for the event. Others, passing by on the highway, stopped to see what was going on. Cars filled the churchyard and lined the road.

Would she never quit looking for Cole? Amanda asked herself in exasperation, while she smiled sweetly at a gray-haired gentleman and sold him a plate of brownies. Still, her eyes scanned the crowd, looking for the familiar dark head.

She spotted Dan and returned his smile. A few minutes later Dan's young son, Jimmy, slipped up beside her and tugged at her skirt, grinning. "Which basket is yours, Amanda?"

Amanda smiled. "I'm not going to tell you, Jimmy. It's secret."

"Can't you give me a hint? Daddy's counting on me."

"Okay," Amanda said with a sigh. "Do you like daisies?"

"I think so," Jimmy said slowly, thinking. He brightened. "I bet Daddy does."

"Well, so do I," Amanda said.

Jimmy attempted a wink, then skipped away. Amanda's heart warmed as she watched his slight form. He was such a loving little boy. He and Amanda had hit it off from the start. Then, thinking of Dan, she vowed to make sure they ate the lunch among a group of other people.

Since the weather was balmy, the auction for both the quilts and the ladies' lunches was held from the back end of Lowry Loggin's pickup. Lowry acted as the official auctioneer. He maintained this right because he'd done it for the past fifteen years. "And," Lowry declared, "I'll not have anybody else getting Mae's lunch. We all know she's the best cook in the county!" He plopped several bills in the jar to start the auction rolling.

Amanda stood with the other women while the wide knot of men behind the truck made their bids for each lunch. Dan caught her eye and winked. Amanda smiled back softly and wondered what in the world she was going to do.

When Lowry held Amanda's basket high, Dan's voice rang out loud and clear with a generous bid. Amanda was about ready to step forward, when another voice sounded— a deep gruff voice calling out a counter bid.

Startled, Amanda scanned the crowd. She knew it had been Cole's voice, but she couldn't see him. Dan, too, was taken aback. Quickly he bid again. A buzz went through the crowd, and Amanda felt herself the object of rapt attention. The heat crept to her face, but she strove to look totally impassive.

Again Cole's voice made a counter bid, upping the price by ten dollars this time. Lowry looked to Dan, and Dan answered strongly.

Amanda wished fervently that the ground would open up and swallow her as chuckles sounded through the crowd. Her emotions were a battleground. Half of her was furious with Cole for putting her in this position, and the other half was so thrilled she could hardly keep from jumping up and down.

Swiftly Cole matched and raised Dan's bid. Amanda's eyes widened and she thought that surely she'd been mistaken. Was the amount up to seventy dollars? Surely it couldn't be. Dan bid again—eighty dollars. Half the people stared at her, the other half at Cole, waiting.

"Well, Cole, what do you say?" Lowry asked.

Oh, bid, you stubborn, stubborn man, Amanda thought. Then, *No, no, oh, I don't know what I want!* She chewed her lip and stood rooted to the spot, trying very hard not to look at anyone. She couldn't help glancing at Dan, and saw Ricky step up beside him and speak into his ear.

"One hundred dollars," Cole called out.

Amanda sucked in her breath along with everyone else and knew for certain her face was a deep beet-red.

All eyes turned to Dan. He argued with Ricky a moment, then threw up his hands. Stepping back from the crowd, he called up to Lowry, "I have to go. Emergency call!" He cast Amanda a look somewhere between anger and apology, then gave it one last try. "One hundred and ten!"

"One hundred and twenty!" Cole shouted quickly, and stepped up to the back of the truck, reaching for Amanda's basket. Laughter rang out from the crowd as Cole walked triumphantly over to take Amanda's hand. She felt rather like she'd been laid claim to and hesitated while she stared heatedly up into Cole's twinkling brown eyes. Eyes which dared her.

Coolly, with every bit of dignity she could muster, Amanda allowed Cole to lead her from the crowd. When they approached his truck, she stopped.

"There's plenty of space right here to eat," she said firmly. "I'm not getting in that truck and going off with you. For heaven's sake! What would everyone say after the display you've just put on?"

"It's too crowded here," Cole answered pleasantly, opening the cab door. "And since when did Amanda Jameson give two hoots about what people would say?" Setting the lunch basket on the seat, he pushed it far over on the passenger side. "Are you going to get in, or am I going to liven things up more by lifting you in?" He smiled.

Amanda's eyes widened. "You wouldn't."

"Try me," he dared, and by the mischievous look in his eyes, Amanda knew he would. "Now, how would it look, you auctioning your lunch for a worthy charity and then refusing to follow through with the tradition of eating with the buyer?"

Amanda closed her eyes and took a deep breath, knowing she was bested and mortified by the entire situation—yet unable to keep her heart from singing. Cole didn't move as she stepped under his arm that held the truck door wide. With the basket on the seat, Amanda was forced to sit in the middle. Cozy, it must look to the goodly number of people who still watched, Amanda thought.

As Cole backed and turned to pull onto the road, Amanda thought of Dan. She felt terribly guilty because she wasn't one bit sorry that it was Cole sitting beside her.

Chapter Eleven

Cole drove north along the blacktopped state highway. After a few minutes Amanda said, "How did you know which lunch was mine?"

"Maybe I wasn't bidding on your lunch. Maybe I was just bidding on *a* lunch and it turned out to be yours." He glanced at her.

"You were sure determined to get *that* lunch."

"Well, I figured the good doctor wanted it pretty badly. Maybe he knew something I didn't." Cole shifted into low and turned east down a gravel road.

"Just where are we going?"

"A nice, peaceful place for a picnic." Cole drove on and Amanda said nothing else. The road rolled up and down several hills until it came to flat bottomland. Plowed fields stretched away on either side. Cole followed the road down to a river with a wide sandy floodplain. The road appeared to go right across the wide, shallow-looking stream of water and to continue on the other side.

"Caddo Jake's Crossing," Cole said, slowly guiding the truck down onto the flat damp sand of the riverbed. There were several trucks already parked to the side, and a cluster of people, picnickers in lawn chairs, gathered near the water's edge.

"You're going to drive the river?" Amanda asked, mystified. From where she sat, the depth looked uncertain and the water flowed rapidly.

"Sure."

And he did. The water splashed the sides of the truck as Cole eased it into the river, searching for the shallowest parts. He turned away from the picnickers and drove until he came to a wide expanse of white sand dunes, sparkling in the sun, and dotted here and there with bushes. Tall cottonwoods bordered the floodplain and they, too, showed signs of new life. It was exceedingly quiet when Cole cut the engine—quiet and peaceful. They were very much alone. Amanda looked at Cole, but he was already half out of the truck.

"I didn't pack a picnic cloth." Amanda got out of the truck, feeling very rebellious. He'd brought her out here against her will. High-handed again. Her mind argued that she wanted to be with him, but she didn't want to admit it— not to Cole. Not even to herself. It was too risky, too much pain was involved.

"I did." Cole said, reaching into the large tool chest in the back of the pickup and pulling out a plaid blanket. He spread it on the ground, and while Amanda continued to stand with her arms crossed, he got the basket from the cab.

Amanda sat on the blanket, and Cole placed the basket between them. "I believe you're supposed to serve." He smiled with self-satisfaction. "Let's see what the good doctor was so eager to buy."

She handed him a plate, taking one herself. "I don't like the way you refer to Dan. And you embarrassed him back there, bidding like that."

"It was an auction. People are supposed to bid against each other. And it is for charity, after all." Lifting the foil covering the pie, Cole sniffed appreciatively. "How'd you know I love raisin pie?"

"Dan likes it," she said, pushing his hand away, covering the dish again. "And right now he doesn't have the kind of money to spare that you forced the bidding up to. He's recently moved here, opening a practice, and has a child to support. You forced him, Cole. Who knows how high he would have kept going if he hadn't been called away?"

"But he didn't have to go higher," Cole said. "And anyway, I intended to win."

She looked directly into his brown eyes, and they shifted nervously as a slight grin played upon his lips. Suspicion tugged at Amanda, and she remembered Ricky murmuring in Dan's ear.

"What did you put Ricky up to?"

"Let's just say I saved the good doctor a bit of money— and myself besides." Shifting his eyes, he helped himself to potato salad.

Amanda jerked the bowl from his reach. "There wasn't any emergency, was there? You had Ricky go over and make up something to tell Dan. Ricky! You're supposed to be a good influence on him, Cole Mattox!"

"I am a good influence on him—most of the time. Besides, he wanted to help. We could still be there bidding. The doctor is a stubborn man. And as you pointed out, he can't afford it." His eyes twinkled mightly. "He'll get paid for tending my brother's sick cow."

Amanda shut her mouth and stared at him. He had been determined to win. Determined to have lunch with her. It

was almost too much to take in. Why? He'd barely said two
words to her in the past two months. He could have seen her
anytime; they could have had lunch, dinner. Why today?

She sat across from him and silently picked at her food
wondering about her heart—and about Cole's.

"I used to come here a lot as a kid," Cole remarked. "It's
a good place to shoot snakes and ride dirt bikes. The river's
a bit high now, will get a lot higher in late spring. During the
heavy rains, this river can rise in a flash. See how it cuts into
the sand." He pointed to the far bank where the earth had
been sheared off, leaving a dirt wall about four feet high
showing exposed tree roots.

Amanda listened as Cole spoke between bites. And she
watched him. The bright daylight was reflected in his deep
brown eyes, and an urge assailed her to touch his hair. It
would feel warm from the sunshine.

"It's a great place for picnics," Amanda said. "Do you
come here often now?"

He studied her a minute. "You mean, do I bring many
women down here?"

Amanda blinked. That was what she'd meant.

Cole gave a wry laugh. "You think I'm a wicked man
with the ladies, don't you, Amanda? That I hop in and out
of bed all over the place."

Amanda shrugged. "Well, I've sure noticed you with a lot
of women, and your approach to me was anything but
standoffish. Most men nowadays..."

"I'm not most men," Cole clipped, helping her clear the
dishes and replace things in the basket. A moment later he
touched her chin and forced her to look at him. "I don't
play around, Manda. I tired of that a long time ago. Besides the numerous dangers, it has no meaning." He
dropped his hand. His eyes looked sad; his voice reflected
disappointment.

Silence stretched between them. Amanda finished the re-
packing while Cole stretched the length of the blanket.
Propping his head with his hand, he watched her intently,
giving every indication of staying indefinitely.

She closed the basket, then pulled out the decorative
daisies one by one. Their stems were limp now, much like
wet green noodles. Stretching them across her lap, Amanda
brushed wisps of hair from her temple and asked softly,
"Why did you do this? Why?" She raised her eyes to his.

His eyes reflected a mixture of confusion and, perhaps,
guilt. He reached out, closed his rough hand around her
wrist and tugged her toward him. At first Amanda resisted.
Then her eyes met his and she went willingly to lie beside
him. She could feel the heat from his body.

She lay flat against the blanket, Cole's head above her
own. Lifting one of the limp daisies that were scattered
around, he brushed the white petals softly against her cheek,
his eyes seeking hers, questioning her. Then he tossed the
flower to the sand and stroked the wisps of hair surrounding her face. The action sent shivers of delight slipping down
Amanda's limbs.

"You do that whenever you're nervous," Cole said, his
gravelly voice barely above a whisper. "You brush those few
hairs. Did you know that? I noticed it that first night—the
night you looked so much like a raccoon."

Amanda simply stared into his deep, fathomless brown
eyes. She couldn't look away, didn't want to, any more than
she wanted to lose the warm, lazy, delicious feeling welling
up within her. His face was so close his breath caressed her
skin. She touched her fingertips to his soft beard. Though
she didn't repeat the question, it hung there between them.

"I don't know why I did it." Cole's warm gaze shifted to
her hair. "Maybe it was your hair." His finger touched her
lips. "Maybe it was those lips." His tone dropped lower and

his eyes clouded. "I don't know why. I hadn't even meant to stop at the bazaar. I just couldn't stand the thought of you going off with the doctor for a picnic, of him being the one lying with you on a blanket in the sun."

Amanda watched his eyes move to her neck. He lightly stroked the sensitive skin there with his fingers. His hand moved, languidly tracing a line low on her neck, his eyes following. Closing her eyes, Amanda drew in a deep breath and arched her neck, reveling in the sensation like a cat that loves to be scratched.

Slowly, almost tentatively, Cole smoothed his hand over one breast, down to her ribs, the curve of her waist and to the swell of her thigh. Amanda's whole body tingled with his touch, coming to life.

He rested his hand on her waist and it felt hot, as if there wasn't a thread of fabric separating it from her skin. Still her fingers rested against his beard while she looked at him in wonder. Hesitantly she moved her fingers to touch his hair. It was sun warmed as she'd imagined. They were so close; electricity vibrated and crackled between them. Cole's body exuded warmth and his chest rose and fell in a soft rhythm. He smelled of after-shave, cotton flannel and sunshine. The hand he rested on her waist remained very still, conspicuously so.

Amanda wanted the moment to last forever, to capture it and put it in a bottle where she could look through the glass and see it from all angles. She looked at him in wonder, impressing upon her memory the deep brown crystal of his eyes, the way his brows grew softly together and the uncommon smoothness of his skin above his beard.

There was a feeling between them that went beyond words. It was a knowing, intimately, of one another.

Never had she experienced such feelings, and he knew it; she could see this in his eyes. Just by looking at her, Cole knew how she felt. And his eyes, too, reflected a wonderment, a fascination, as he gazed down at her.

Time stopped, suspended just for them. A gentle breeze tugged at her hair and a bobwhite called from the field beyond the trees. Around her everything sparkled with light, but Cole's head blocked the sun, and her eyes caressed his face.

Her breath grew rapid and shallow, and she watched the heat gather in Cole's eyes. Still she rested one hand on his hair, the other at her side. She dared not move, for the energy that entwined them was on the verge of exploding. She didn't know...feared, yet didn't fear. Cole, too, remained motionless and his hand seemed to burn into her.

Then, in measured slow motion, Cole lowered his head. Amanda closed her eyes, and as though by instinct, her lips parted, welcoming his kiss and the thrust of his tongue.

His lips were warm and tender, seeking a response. Heated honey stole through her body. Her arms, legs—all over—felt deliciously heavy. Cole drew back, then kissed her again, this time hard, seeking, demanding. Amanda wrapped her arms around his neck, melding herself to him.

She loved this man and every bit of her, body, mind and soul, sought to sing it out. Amanda savored the feeling, marveling at its exquisite beauty while her heart swelled with emotions tumbling over themselves.

She felt the cords in Cole's neck, the strength of him, the silkiness of his hair. He kissed her cheek and the sensitive skin down to the hollow of her neck. Her breath was gone, blown away with the breeze, and her mind, a colorful whirl as Cole's strong frame pressed against her.

An intense longing tugged at her and she moved with every touch of Cole's hand against her skin. It was a strong, firm touch, at the same time conveying supreme tenderness. Closer...she wanted to be as close as possible....

Then she heard an alarm within the whirling, something tugging her back, though she really didn't want to come back. Not yet...oh, not yet. Cole's hand was hot upon her skin, the bare skin of her stomach beneath her blouse, her ribs, his thumb stroking upward beneath her bra. Her breasts tingled in anticipation...wanting... It felt so very good, and she wanted to feel his touch all over.

Amanda stiffened as she felt Cole's muscles tighten and his body grow very still, his chest barely even moving. A coldness invaded her bones, bringing her back to the moment, leaving her confused and aching.

Cole didn't move. His lips were brushing her ear, his beard soft against her cheek. Amanda wasn't sure who was trembling, she or Cole. Then she realized it was both of them. Slowly Cole pulled his hand from her stomach and smoothed her blouse. He did not look at her, and a tear squeezed from her eye. She was so confused. And he was pulling away, mentally as well as physically, building an invisible shield around himself. She wanted to call aloud to him, "Don't go." But she couldn't.

Cole sat up, his back to her.

"I'm sorry," he said huskily.

Amanda sat up and curled her legs beneath her skirt.

"I'm not." The words came out husky. Cole turned to look at her. "I feel no shame in desiring you." She tilted her chin upward, realizing she was again brushing the hair from her face. "And I'm not sorry we stopped. I'm not sorry for thinking of giving myself to you as something so precious that I want it to happen at a special time, a special place. I want it to mean something to you," she said, barely above a whisper. "So which are you sorry for? That you want to make love to me or that you stopped?"

Cole sat there looking at her, his eyes speculative. "You drive me crazy, woman." His gruff voice vibrated with emotion.

"What are we going to do about it?"

"We aren't going to do anything." Cole stood up. "I'm taking you home."

"Cole." Amanda shot him an imploring glance as she stood to face him. She remained on the blanket so he couldn't pick it up. "What's between us—you can't just deny it any longer."

"Get off the blanket, Amanda."

"No." She clenched her hands.

Smoldering anger as well as a hint of pain showed in Cole's eyes.

"Why did you bring me out here today? What was the whole meaning of that charade you pulled back at the church?"

"I went crazy, okay?" He spoke harshly. "I wasn't thinking. There's no way we can be together and things not get out of hand. I was fooling myself if I thought we could."

"I love you, Cole," Amanda stated very quietly.

Cole looked down at the sand for several seconds, then back at her. "How can you be so sure?"

"I just know."

"What do you want from me, Amanda?" A coldness touched his voice and invaded Amanda's heart. His eyes glittered down at her. "Look at me—really look at me. I've seen and done things—things that make me light-years from your world. I haven't been to church in ages. I don't fit, and I don't care to fit into that established type of life. I can't quite see myself playing the organ for you in church," he said scornfully. "Isn't that what the spouse of the minister does? And what about tea parties? I don't make cake. I don't sew or bake or do anything else a pastor's spouse is supposed to do."

Anger, humiliation and despair rose in Amanda. "I don't think of you as being a pastor's husband. I think of you as..." She stopped, fear welling in her at what she really dreamed of, really wanted, knowing the hurt of rejection. She forced her voice lower. "I am a woman and I want to be a woman to you, not a pastor. That's how I think of you. And, yes, I want womanly things such as marriage and children."

Cole looked at her a long moment before saying, "Let's go."

That was all. She was being dismissed like an errant child. Amanda swallowed, willing her eyes to remain dry. She slipped into the far side of the passenger seat and tried to console herself, with common platitudes such as: keep an open mind; it's for the best; everything will work out.

But she didn't believe any of it. She was hurt and angry. Her heart was breaking; her body betraying her. She didn't want to be calm and rational. Her body throbbed in longing for the man who sat so very near, and it was taking all he had, just to keep from screaming.

The sun sat low on the horizon when they pulled in front of her house. Amanda looked at Cole quizzically when he reached for her hand. Thoughtfully he rubbed his thumb over her own.

"I really care for you, Manda. Maybe I even love you. But I'm just not the man for you."

Somehow, she found her voice, though it came out raspy. "You asked me to look at you, really look. Well I have over these last months, and I see a man, one I have great respect for. I see a man who creates beauty and comfort with his hands, a kind, strong man, with deep feelings, who cares for

others. A man who makes me feel very much a woman an
very glad to be alive."

She waited, but Cole said nothing. Quietly she slippe
from the truck before he could see her face. She walke
quickly up the stairs and in the door. Minutes later sh
heard Cole's heavy footsteps on the porch and her hear
leaped into her throat. But then she realized he was onl
leaving the picnic basket, and a minute later he drove away
Truly, truly, her heart was breaking and she'd never felt suc
pain in all her life.

The next morning, Amanda drank five cups of coffee an
geared herself up to face the congregation and to delive
what she hoped would at least be a halfway decent sermon
People were depending on her. Pastors were expected to b
the rock other people could turn to, dump their problem
and their joys on.

But I'm a woman, too, she thought sadly. I'm lost, alone
confused. Damn you, Cole Mattox! After an inner strug
gle, her calm, good sense returned, if a bit scarred. This
too, would pass.

As she entered the church, she smiled, though perhaps
bit too brightly, and ignored the curious glances of thos
who were thinking about the auction and Cole Mattox'
determined bidding. She talked happily and appeared per
fectly normal. Mae Loggin, though, knew her entirely to
well, and cast Amanda a concerned look, but said nothing

Then suddenly, there before her, stood Cole. Amanda fel
as if she'd been punched in the stomach as he politely hel
his hand out to shake hers.

"Good morning, Pastor." He wore a western-style cor
duroy coat and matching slacks. Amanda thought she'
never seen him look so handsome.

I've put you out of my mind, she thought, her mind re-
pelling. What in the world was he doing here?

Others were watching. "Good morning, Cole." She refused to say Mr. Mattox. He grinned and her heart tugged.
Why? Why was he here?

Cole didn't sit in the front pew, but he might as well have.
His presence seemed to captivate the room. Amanda wondered if the hum of whispers she heard were really louder
than normal, or if she were inordinately sensitive. To mag-
nify her discomfort, Dan repeatedly cast Cole dark glances.
Oh, Lord, don't let there be another brawl right here, she
thought sinkingly.

Her gaze moved across the room. Ricky, Mae, Pa Hammond, Emily, Glenda—everyone's eyes seemed to dance
with expectation. She felt people were watching her so
closely, they could see her pink lace bra and panties.

She gave her shortest sermon ever. When she ended, there
were many surprised faces in the congregation. Amanda just
hoped she'd made sense. Her mind had kept straying, re-
calling Cole's kisses, their argument of the day before and
her firm intention to put him out of her thoughts, out of her
life.

Amanda stood at the door as on every Sunday and greeted
people as they filed out of the church. For some unfath-
omable reason, Cole came to stand beside her. He shook
hands as well. "Good to see you here, Cole." "Been a long
time, Cole." "Real fine work on the south wing, Cole. I
need to see you about an addition to our house." Cole
smiled with impeccable politeness, answering smoothly.
Glances alive with curiosity flickered from Cole to Amanda
and people seemed content to mill around in the churchyard longer than usual and whispers abounded.

Amanda, at a loss for what was going on, tried simply to
get through the moments and hoped she appeared sane.

Then Dan was there, his small son running ahead out the door. Dan took Cole's outstretched hand. "I owe you one." The words were spoken with a wry friendliness. He took Amanda's hand. "Good day, Amanda." It sounded more like "Goodbye."

"Dan..." But she really didn't have anything to say. "Thank you."

Before everyone had left, Cole slipped away. Amanda, watching him walk to his truck, had a strong urge to run after him, curious onlookers or no, but restrained herself. She didn't want to embarrass him by making a spectacle of the situation. Later, alone in the parsonage, she cursed her stupidity. What did it matter what people said? She should have gone after him and found out what in the world he was thinking.

Maybe he didn't know. Maybe he was as confused as she. Surely he would call.

He didn't that night, and Amanda refused to call him.

But in the small hours of the morning, she decided she'd had enough. And she didn't care if she woke him up. She turned on the bedside lamp and reached for the telephone. Five times the ring sounded, but there was no answer. Aggravated, Amanda replaced the receiver. Not home? For heaven's sake! Maybe he was just a sound sleeper. Well, there was tomorrow.

Chapter Twelve

The wind rose in the night, hard. Amanda heard it as she lay awake. Finally she fell asleep, and when she woke the sun was high behind a thin layer of clouds. A pinkish haze of blowing dirt covered the sky. Wet wind approached from the south, while dryer, cold air bore down from the north. The combination was sure to bring a heavy spring storm.

After breakfast Amanda picked up her keys and headed for the Jeep. Halfway down the walk, she changed her mind and turned around, stomped into the house and slammed the door behind her.

Amanda Jameson did not chase after some bullheaded man. If he wanted her, he knew where she was. Casting the telephone a dark stare, she resolutely turned away.

Just as soon as she could figure out what to say, she would call Bishop Henderson and request a transfer. Or a leave of absence. Anything. Only she had to leave. She couldn't handle this thing any longer. She felt a pang of guilt, thinking of her church, the people. But she just had to. Running away. Yes, it was running away, and she was going to get to it as soon as possible.

She busied herself cleaning the house. Anger threatened to best her every time she thought of the situation. Her heart was heavy and her mind dark as she started polishing the furniture, finding herself doing one spot over and over.

It was late afternoon when she became aware of the wind becoming even stronger. The front bearing down from the north had met the winds from the south. The winds seemed to do battle right over her house. Amanda watched out the window, fascinated by the boiling clouds and the giant raindrops that began to fall.

Even as she watched, to the southwest, a pale gray shape dropped from the clouds. It looked rather like a dog's tail whooshing back and forth. With a catch in her throat, Amanda realized it was a funnel cloud, its tip touching the ground— bearing toward Coogan!

She grabbed for the telephone, then realized there simply wasn't time. The noise of the wind grew even higher. Dropping the receiver, she headed out the back door for the storm shelter. The rain beat at her head as she struggled with the old wooden door, opened it and held to it as she went down the steps. The wind threatened to rip the door from her hands, but at last it thudded closed, and she was in darkness. She stood still a moment and waited for her eyes to adjust, wishing she'd had forethought enough to keep a lantern down here. Gradually the darkness paled. Enough gray light filtered through the air vent for Amanda to see somewhat.

Amanda sat in the dark shelter, water dripping from her hair onto her nose, her shoulders shaking, and feeling much like a miserably wet dog.

She wondered if it truly had been a tornado. It seemed odd that she'd lived so much of her life in the state and had never actually seen one—not up close and threatening. The wind wailed above. Amanda thought of the many people she knew who lived close by: Mae and Lowry, Mary and Roy—and Cole.

Though she could still hear heavy rain on the shelter door, Amanda detected a drop in the wind. Other than a few creaks and groans of the shelter door, she heard little else.

Cautiously she raised the door and looked around while rain poured like buckets upon her head.

Heavy clouds hung above and lightning crackled. Water ran in rivulets around the shelter and out through the yard, which was strewn with broken tree branches. The trees still swayed, but the wind was gradually dropping. The house was untouched. Water rushed from all the gutters.

She ran up onto the back deck. From there she could see several trees uprooted in the wood to the south. Her heart leaped in her throat, and she had to know—she had to find out if Cole was all right. In her mind she saw his trailer turned over and mangled. Running soggily through the house, she grabbed her keys and sprinted for the Jeep.

Still the rain poured. It coursed down her drive, and the the road in front of her house resembled a muggy river of red clay. The Jeep managed, though. With the windshield wipers whipping back and forth, Amanda strained to see through the rain as she headed toward Cole's place.

An old and rotted tree had fallen, covering half the road. Carefully Amanda drove around it. On the other side she came upon Cole's truck turned on its side. Water and sludgy orange mud oozed down the road, banking up around the truck, sucking at it and seeming to inch the truck along with it, and all of it damming up against the fallen tree.

Amanda clawed for the door handle and stumbled out into the wet and the mud. With her head bowed against the rain, she fairly lurched her way through the mud, which sucked at her feet. Her heart pounded in her chest.

"Cole!" she screamed. "Cole!"

Cole had slept in his house that night. He had his bed and dishes moved in and running water and electricity, but the telephone was still over in his trailer. He didn't mind about the telephone anyway because he wanted to be alone with no interruptions while he worked and thought out exactly what he wanted to say to Amanda.

He'd been working on the trim in the kitchen when he heard the change in the wind. It'd not been unexpected. From the window, he saw the snakelike funnel of the tornado, but could also see that it hung above the ground, at treetop level. His next thought was of Amanda, for the funnel was heading toward Coogan, and it could decide to touch the ground anytime.

The gray funnel shape draped downward, its tail licking the taller trees to the east of Cole's house. It lifted, then lowered, again at treetop level. For one strange moment, Cole felt he could almost reach up and touch it as it passed. There came a roaring in the air. Mac whined under the table and the windows rattled, the rain pounded and branches broke against the outside wall. Cole backed into a corner of the house that was protected by a banked dirt wall outside.

Then the wind slackened. Cole didn't waste any time. He had to get to Amanda and make sure she was all right. What if she were hurt or worse?

The sandy-clay road had become a flowing mire. The truck slid from side to side as Cole went as fast as possible. As he drove, he searched the woods for any sign that the whirling wind had touched down. Thankfully, there was none, just broken and fallen trees here and there.

Then Cole saw one of those trees up ahead blocking part of the road. He felt the thickening mud pull at the wheels of his truck. The next moment, the truck began to slide to the side of the road. It tilted, then everything seemed to happen in slow motion. The truck hung there, its two right wheels sinking into the flowing mud, while the left wheels came up off the firm sandstone in the middle of the road. Cole gunned the engine and pulled at the wheel, certain for a moment that the truck would right itself.

It didn't.

Ever so slowly, as the truck fell to its side, Cole's body slid to the passenger seat, his hands still gripping the steering wheel. Rain ran in sheets across the windshield, pooled on the side window that faced the sky and leaked in measured drips around its edges.

Cole sucked in a deep breath. He listened, thinking he'd heard a car engine. Then he pulled himself up by the steering wheel and managed to wedge his feet against the floor. He rested there, wondering how it had all happened so fast.

For an unbelievable second, he thought he heard Amanda's voice calling his name. He shook his head, thinking he must have hit it or something when the truck turned over. The call came again.

It was her.

Looking out the back window, he saw her face peering in at him. Half her hair had slipped from its braid. It was soaking wet, clinging to her face, plastered down by the rain. Copper-colored mud smudged her right cheek, and her eyes looked hollow in her pale face.

Cole managed to swing the truck door open. It dropped back down, and Amanda yelled, "Wait a minute. I'll get it."

"Just get out of the way!" Cole hollered back, pushing the door again, hard. It swung open and caught straight up, somewhat unsteadily. Rain poured in. Cole clutched the door frame, his grip made slippery by the mud. Mud. It was everywhere.

He heard Amanda's heavy breath.

"Give me your hand," she called in a sobbing voice as her face appeared above him.

"I can manage, Amanda," Cole said, impatiently. "Just get back!" She'd climbed the now sideway pickup bed and was balanced on hands and knees on the side of the truck.

"The door, Cole," she cautioned. "Watch it! It's about to..."

The door slammed into his arm as he tried to haul himself out. Amanda screamed and lunged forward. At the same time Cole pushed himself from the cab.

"Amanda!"

She slipped. The door banged into his back, and Cole grunted as Amanda cried out. Then they both fell from the side of the pickup into the mud.

Clay-orange mud oozed everywhere: sticky, slimy and disgusting. Now that Cole knew Amanda was safe, he was mad as hell. Raising up on his knees, he dragged her from the orangish mire. He held her by the shoulders and shook her. Damn! He'd been scared half out of his wits. And now, because of her foolishness, they were both sitting in the mud, soaking wet and freezing.

"I told you to get back," he yelled. "What are you doing out in this? You could get killed!"

"So could you!" Her eyes flashed. "It isn't my truck stuck on its side in the mud."

The obvious made Cole even angrier.

"I told you to get out of the way. You're a damn fool crazy woman!"

"I'm glad you finally noticed the woman part!" Amanda shot back as she pushed his hands away.

They glared at each other, both kneeling in the mud, while the rain poured on them and the wind whistled in the tree limbs above. Amanda was plastered with mud, her feminine form clearly visible. Cole experienced a pang as it registered: She was all woman. The woman he loved. *Yes, he loved her.*

"I was scared, Amanda!" he hollered as he reached for her, pulling her to him. All he could think was she was here with him now, she was safe. He held her, relief washing over him. He rubbed a muddy hand over her hair and pressed his cheek to hers. "I was afraid you were hurt...that the storm..."

She was in his arms. He was a solid rock against her. Amanda clung to him, as grateful now as she'd been livid a minute before. Cole pulled away and suddenly she felt cold. Struggling to his feet, he helped her up after him, his hand gripping hers like a vise.

"Oh, Cole, your truck," Amanda moaned. The vehicle looked like a ungainly beached whale. Mud had oozed up around the left wheels and into the bed. Its sleek black surface showed only in spots through a film of grime.

She looked at Cole. He stared woefully at the vehicle. Then Amanda realized he'd not let go of her hand, that he was still clenching it tightly in his own. As she looked at him, a chuckle, which she tried to choke down, rumbled in the back of her throat. Cole was plastered with mud. His pants were so coated that not one patch of denim could be seen. She couldn't even tell for certain what color his shirt was. Orange clay splattered his hair and his beard, and the rain traced lines through it all. But still, he was a beautiful sight to her.

Hearing Amanda chuckle, Cole looked at her and grinned. Amanda looked down at her own body and erupted in a full-fledged laugh.

Cole swooped her up in his arms and headed for the Jeep.

"Oh no!" Amanda protested, swinging her feet in the air. "Not the Jeep. The mud, Cole!"

"And what do you suggest? Do you want to walk the two miles to my house through this?" With ease, he juggled her and opened the passenger door at the same time, plopping Amanda on the seat.

Amanda squeezed her eyes shut. The muddy water tickled as it slipped between her breasts and dripped from her body onto the lamb's wool seat cover.

At Cole's house, they ran from the Jeep to the side entrance. Amanda wondered why they bothered to run, since they were already as muddy and wet as they could possibly be.

Cole ushered her into the kitchen, and Amanda looked down at herself, letting out a half moan of dismay. Muddy water dripped wherever she stepped. Mac wagged his tail, but backed away instead of advancing.

Cole reached for her hand. "Come on."

"Cole?" Amanda tugged at his hand, but he pulled her firmly along through the house.

"It'll wash," he growled.

The next moment he flipped on a light and was tugging Amanda right along with him into a bathroom. Amanda didn't know what to expect—wasn't at all sure, but everything was happening so fast, she couldn't do anything. Laughing at her surprised face, he tugged her into the shower, quickly turned a knob and cold water sprayed them both, clothes and all.

"Oh!" Amanda cried when the water hit her head. Laughing she pushed him out of the way and tried to elude the cold stream. Chuckling deeply, he pushed her back, then moved close and let the water spray them both.

"Thought we needed cooling off as well as cleaning," he shouted over the noise of the shower.

The water warmed, and Amanda leaned into it gratefully as it drew the shivers from her body. It ran down their hair and faces, taking the mud with it.

Cole's face was very close. He ran his hands down her back, cupped her buttocks and pulled her against him. Amanda touched her fingers to his beard, its lustrous color returning as the mud disappeared. Reaching up, she stroked the stray hairs from his forehead. A flicker of longing leaped within his cocoa-colored eyes and hungrily his mouth sought hers, forcing her lips to part, taking her breath.

Pulling back, he looked at her for a long moment before he let her go.

"There's a robe on back of the door," he said. Stained water splashed the floor as he stepped from the shower and walked out of the bathroom, softly closing the door behind him.

Amanda stripped and piled her clothes in a corner of the shower stall. She washed, luxuriating in the feel of being clean after all the coarse and sticky mud.

Several minutes later, wrapped in Cole's oversize robe, she hesitantly stepped from the room and padded to the kitchen.

Cole was leaning against the counter. He was dressed now in clean clothes, his shirt hanging open, revealing his strong chest sparsely covered with dark hair. He held out a steaming cup of coffee. As she reached for it, Amanda suddenly remembered when they'd shared coffee in the kitchen of the church—and he'd kissed her for the first time.

"How did you...?" She waved indicating his clean clothes.

"Another shower upstairs."

"Oh..." Amanda took one sip of her coffee, then Cole's work-roughened hand took it from her and set it aside as his other arm closed around her waist and drew her close. Putting her hands against his chest, Amanda rested her head beneath his neck.

He tilted her face, forcing her to look at him. "I love you, Amanda."

"I love you, Cole."

"Do you want lots of kids?"

Her mind clouded. This was his way of talking commitment, marriage. "Why...what made you...was it the storm? I mean..." Oh, she didn't know what she meant. Only she didn't want Cole deciding this based on the emotion of the moment, of the danger that had now passed.

He cupped her face in his rough hands. "I love you, Amanda. Hell, yes, the storm scared me. But I'd already decided that I wanted you. I spent the whole night and today figuring out how I was going to ask you. It was hard, seeing as I felt somewhat of a fool after the last time we were together. Now I see just how simple it really is, though. I want to marry you. I want to live with you, have children with you and even hear you preach. And I want..." He left the rest unsaid, but his intention was written plainly in his eyes.

"Maybe three or four," Amanda replied in a sultry tone.

"Three or four?"

"Children."

A grin tugged at Cole's lips. "That's a lot." His hands moved up and down her back.

"Ummm," Amanda agreed sweetly. "But I'll be a full-time mother."

"You want that?" A furrow creased Cole's brow. "To leave the ministry?"

Amanda nodded. "I think of it simply as a different kind of ministry. I'll have my own family to take care of." She moved her lips close to his. "To love," she whispered.

He pulled her against him hard and buried his face in her damp hair. "I could never learn to play the organ, but we'd adjust just fine if you want to continue in the ministry."

Amanda pulled back and looked at him. Lightly she traced the curve of his soft beard. He was here with her. He loved her. Her heart swelled near to bursting. "Thank you. There's time for that later."

Cole grinned, and a tingling slipped down Amanda's spine. "We'd better get started if you want that many kids, Manda. Neither of us is getting any younger."

And then he kissed her. A deep kiss, setting her blood flowing and filling her with excitement. She pressed against him, wanting to get as close as possible, feeling him firm and hard against her.

Then—"Tomorrow?" he growled, breaking away, his eyes heavy with desire.

Amanda looked at him. Tomorrow seemed an eternity away. They were here now.

He set her from him. "Tomorrow, Manda."

"Yes," she agreed, smiling into his warm eyes.

"I don't want you trying to get home on these roads," Cole said. "I want you here with me."

And Amanda wanted to be with him. They talked long into the night and then Amanda lay in Cole's bed thinking what the next night would bring. She smiled in the darkness remembering his gentle touch when he'd stroked her cheek and said in his gravelly voice, "Get upstairs, Manda. We can wait a few more hours to have our dream." He was a strong man, all man. Her body warmed even now as she remembered his muscular shoulders and the smoothness of the skin on his back.

With one look in his eyes, she'd scampered away, pausing in the hall to look back. With her heart beating rapidly, she'd scurried up the stairs, joy flooding through every part of her.

Feeling the empty space beside her, she drifted into sleep, dreaming of the times when Cole would lie beside her and warm the bed with his body.

Then a strange, almost imperceptible fear tugged at her heart, but she pushed it aside and slept.

By eight o'clock the next evening Amanda Jameson had become Amanda Mattox and was alone with Cole at his house. Their house, she corrected herself.

She heard Cole moving in the kitchen below. Her heart thudded rapidly, and again she puzzled over the nameless anxiety that tugged at her.

In the low light of the bedroom she looked at the wedding band glimmering on her finger. She could scarcely take it all in. Was it just that morning they had picked the ring out? Surely it had been months ago.

The day had been a flurry of activity from the moment the sun peeked in the window, awakening Amanda. It was almost as if the tornado of the day before had touched down and blown her into another life. She'd not had time to think, hardly even to feel, except for delightful excitement every time she looked into Cole's warm eyes.

A tremor had passed through her several times, an unrecognizable fear. Bride's jitters, she had consoled herself. It will pass.

She'd worn her mother's wedding gown, still a bit wrinkled after the hurried pressing it had received. Mae had played a love song on the organ, and Cole's parents, two brothers, Billy and Corey, and a sister, Megan, had sat in the front pew with Amanda's mother. Her father performed the ceremony—a ceremony he considered far too hasty and

vasn't very happy about. But then, he knew Amanda would
do as she chose.

They'd left the church in a shower of rice and had one
horrible moment when they thought the truck would stick
in the still mucky road. But they'd made it out. Cole had
driven down the highway as though they were going away to
some secret honeymoon spot. Then they'd doubled back to
his house unseen.

Now they were alone.

Amanda touched the nightgown Mae had given her. Mae
must have bought it long ago. Amanda shook her head at
Mae's forethought. The neckline scooped down across her
breast and the white silky sheer material flowed around her
body touching her skin with a cool richness. Amanda had
never felt so thoroughly feminine in all her life.

She moved toward the fireplace, watching the small
flickering blaze. It was warm for a fire, but Cole had laid it
anyway. Her gaze moved over the room, quite empty yet,
coming to rest on the wide expanse of bed. She'd turned the
covers down, and it lay waiting. Again the strange fear
clutched her heart and her stomach fluttered. She took a
deep breath.

When Cole's footsteps sounded on the stairs, Amanda's
gaze flew to the doorway. He stood there, smiling slightly,
looking at her. His gaze moved very deliberately from her
head to her feet, lingering at several points in between.

The fear knotted in her stomach, paralyzing her.

Crossing the room slowly, Cole drew her to him and
kissed her deeply, then pulled back and looked into her eyes.
A furrow creased his brow. Amanda found herself shaking
and the unnamed fear clawed at her throat. She couldn't get
her breath, and her heart pounded in her ears.

Two desires battled for control within her: one part of her wanted to press herself into the safety of Cole's strong arms, the other part wanted to run, couldn't stand his touch.

"Amanda?" Cole asked softly, puzzlement reflected in his eyes. "What is it?"

She couldn't answer. Her eyes simply stared fearfully into his. When she moved away, she stared at the bed.

I'm thirty years old. What a dumb thing to think at this moment.

"Amanda? What is it?" His fingers pressed into the soft flesh of her upper arms.

She tried to put the fear into words. "I . . . I don't know anything about this, Cole." It sounded absurd out loud. Embarrassed, she turned away. "I'm a thirty-year-old woman and I feel so stupidly ignorant and inept. I . . ." She broke off.

How did she say that she didn't know the first thing about making love and was suddenly, unexplainably, terrified of failing? Oh, for heaven's sake! She didn't know. She risked a glance at Cole. He'd turned his back, and was staring into the fire. His shoulders looked so very rigid, and they shook slightly.

Minutes ticked by. She touched his arm, worried that he was terribly angry with her.

"Cole?" he didn't turn around, but she felt his arm muscle twitch. "Cole?" She pulled at him then. He was . . . why *he was laughing!*

The sound of bubbling laughter rumbled up from him.

Her eyes widened as she watched him. He thought it so funny. Well, she didn't!

Watching her, his laughter faded, replaced by a look of gentle concern. "Ah, Manda." He stretched out his hand to her. Slowly, hesitantly, Amanda placed her hand in his. His strong fingers closed around hers, and he gently drew her close. "Who do you think I am?" he asked in a low voice. "Some Romeo needing to be pleased by a woman skilled in the ways of passion?" His laughter came softly, and Amanda smiled at his words, her fears melting away like frost under the morning sun.

"I guess we do have a lot to learn about each other." She rested her head against his hard chest.

"Yes," he said. "And it'll take a lifetime." Tenderly his hand stroked and kneaded her back.

Her blood grew warm, her body throbbed. His hands moved lower, pressing her against his hardness. A tingling joy filled her being.

The next moment, Cole scooped her into his arms. He looked at her for a long minute, his eyes hot and promising.

Lifetime, Amanda thought as he laid her gently on the bed.

Then he kissed her, at first softly nibbling her lips, then fully claiming them as his own. His strong hand slipped within her gown and tenderly explored her skin. Her heart sang out with love as she gave herself to him, delighting in the feel of his body against her own. Eagerly and completely she lost herself into one of creation's greatest wonders: the love between a woman and a man.

Take 4
Silhouette Special Edition novels
FREE...

and preview future books in your home for 15 days!

Start with 4 FREE books, yours to keep. Then, preview 6 brand-new Special Edition® novels—delivered right to your door every month—as soon as they are published.

When you decide to keep them, pay just $1.95 each ($2.50 each in Canada), *with no shipping, handling, or other additional charges of any kind!*

Romance *is* alive, well and flourishing in the moving love stories presented by Silhouette Special Edition. They'll awaken your desires, enliven your senses, and leave you tingling all over with excitement. In each romance-filled story you'll live and breathe the emotions of love and the satisfaction of romance triumphant.

You won't want to miss a single one of the heartfelt stories presented by Silhouette Special Edition; and when you take advantage of this special offer, you won't have to.

You'll also receive a FREE subscription to the Silhouette Books Newsletter as long as you remain a member. Each lively issue is filled with news on upcoming titles, interviews with your favorite authors, even their favorite recipes.

To become a home subscriber and receive your first 4 books FREE, fill out and mail the coupon today!

Silhouette Special Edition®

Silhouette Books, 120 Brighton Rd., P.O. Box 5084, Clifton, NJ 07015-5084

Silhouette Special Edition

AMERICAN TRIBUTE

Where a man's dreams count for more than his parentage...

Look for these upcoming titles under the Special Edition American Tribute banner.

LOVE'S HAUNTING REFRAIN
Ada Steward #289–February 1986
For thirty years a deep dark secret kept them apart—King Stockton made his millions while his wife, Amelia, held everything together. Now could they tell their secret, could they admit their love?

THIS LONG WINTER PAST
Jeanne Stephens #295–March 1986
Detective Cody Wakefield checked out Assistant District Attorney Liann McDowell, but only in his leisure time. For it was the danger of Cody's job that caused Liann to shy away.

AM-TRIB-1

Silhouette ❤ *Romance*

COMING NEXT MONTH

TO CATCH A THIEF—Brittany Young
Michal went to Paris with one intention—to steal back her
grandmother's chalices that were auctioned off to Frenchman
Phillippe Dumas. She hired a "professional" thief—who ended
up stealing her heart.

WILD HORIZONS—Frances Lloyd
Returning to Australia to claim ownership of his family's outback
ranch. Chad planned to claim Marla, as well. But what about the
scandal that had forced him to leave ten years ago?

YESTERDAY'S HERO—Debbie Macomber
Nothing would keep Leah or Cain from missing an expedition to
study the ancient whales of the Diamantina Islands. But why
would a business trip have to include marriage?

ROSES NEVER FADE—Raye Morgan
In the middle of a stormy northern California night, a handsome
stranger walked into the foyer of Bailey Trent's supposedly
haunted house. He was certainly no ghost, but who was he?

A MAN OF CHARACTER—Barbara Bartholomew
While running the family farm, Cath was quickly falling for
Doug. He was no typical farmhand . . . but he was very
mysterious. What had happened in his past that he was refusing
to reveal?

ANGEL AND THE SAINT—Emilie Richards
Angelle and Kyle had nothing in common, except that each were
trying to adopt an orphaned child. But an earthly act of love
might turn into a marriage made in heaven.

AVAILABLE THIS MONTH: